Also by Alison Leslie Gold

ANNE FRANK REMEMBERED
with Miep Gies

Clairvoyant

Clairvoyant

The Imagined Life
of Lucia Joyce

A Novel by

Alison Leslie Gold

Hyperion   New York

Library of Congress Cataloging-in-Publication Data

Gold, Alison Leslie.
Clairvoyant : the imagined life of Lucia Joyce : a novel / by
Alison Leslie Gold, co-author of Anne Frank remembered.
p. cm.
ISBN 1-56282-986-6 : $19.95
1. Joyce, Lucia, d. 1982—Fiction.   I. Title.
PS3557.03267C57 1992   91-32411
813'.54—dc20   CIP

Book design by Margaret M. Wagner

First Edition

10 9 8 7 6 5 4 3 2 1

To Nurse A.G. Kennedy
of Dublin and New York.

Contents

"My father says that he and I are cut from the same cloth, do you agree, Herr Doktor Jung?"

"Yes," replied Herr Doktor, "you are both like people sinking to the bottom of the same river."

"Then why am I locked up here and why is my father the writer of books?"

"The difference is that you are falling to the bottom of the river and your father is diving."

Clairvoyant

1

At Forty

O N THE rolling lawn of Barnaderg Bay Hospital, the long-term patient known as Miss Lucia Joyce sat in a position of slack repose, in a patch of weak sunlight. Her left wrist was braceleted by a canvas posy, the right by a loose cloth only. Her eyes were shut though the left lid fluttered ever so slightly. Her wavy gingerbread-and-gray hair looked as though it had recently been permed. On her lap lay a small copybook and the stub of a wooden pencil.

A mockingbird trilled from its position on the lower branches of a nearby elm tree. In *entre chat six* the bird leaped into the air, somersaulted, landed on a branch, and then resumed its trilling as it had been doing in tandem to the somersaulting all afternoon a short distance from Miss Joyce's chair.

The faint sun passed behind a cloud, washing a pale shadow across her face. Her right hand jerked against the restraint and lazily she opened both eyes. They were so blue and clear—her mother's eyes she had always been told—that they could almost be regarded as aquamarine. Large drops of rain plopped against the crown of her head.

For a brief moment of ecstasy she smelled the rain-drenched, fresh smell of her mother's wet hair. She waited to hear the tone of her voice. By whether or not it was sharp she would know if her mother had finally forgiven her for being such a disappointment.

The charge nurse, Sister Leary, hurried from inside the greystone chapel, where she had been saying her Rosary. Her face showed concern as the rain began to fall; holding on to her white starched hat, she broke into a run. Reaching the clumsy wheelchair, she hurriedly pushed it across the emerald lawn, Miss Joyce's head bumping as she went.

Miss Joyce showed not the slightest interest in the rain, squinting distractedly at something just out of eye range. Her father had wet her hair with a jug of cool rainwater. Soon he would turn her hair into a halo of soapsuds. His long fingers always made her scalp hum. With the wrong touch, tears of pain sprang to her eyes. While her father sudsed her hair, he would always sing to her in his soft, persuasive Irish tenor voice, his bony body bent over her like a question mark.

She began to hum, her voice sweet but erratic. The bird also trilled noisily.

Her humming continued as Sister Leary ran, barely audible to human ears. Then it trailed off and stopped. The bird grew silent as well.

Sister leaned against the wheelchair in order to push it up the slope into the solarium. She grunted with the effort. Miss Joyce's head rolled backward, her mismatched eyes showing a flicker of alertness, then disinterest.

The solarium was empty except for a woman who had spent her entire adult life at Barnaderg Bay Hospital. She was Mrs. Angeles, often somnambulist, with canine eyes and dust-gray nose, asleep, drooling onto her woolie.

Sister backed Miss Joyce's heavy wheelchair against the wall, beside the horsehair couch with cabbage-flowered coverlet and no-longer-white doilies, embroidered and donated by the church ladies from the nearby village to the Handicapped Children's Home but given by the good sisters there to Barnaderg Bay. Her hair had become wet and tangled.

Mrs. Leary reached under her white starched apron and drew a comb from the pocket of her dark-blue uniform, which was circled by a black belt. At the sight of the comb Miss Joyce recoiled. Mrs. Leary sighed and put the comb away. From the other pocket she removed a packet of Woodbine cigarettes, because she couldn't afford Sweet Aftons until payday. Then a box of wooden matches.

Seeing the cigarettes, Miss Joyce pinned Mrs. Leary with her left eye and Mrs. Leary loosened the right arm restraint. Miss Joyce's remarkably pink and outsize hand closed around the packet.

"Flow gently, Sweet Afton," Miss Joyce teased.

Not one to meet humor with humor, Mrs. Leary sighed once again, "Sorry, dearie, I don't get paid until next week and neither do you." Mrs. Leary gave her a pat on her reddish curls. "I promise, dearie."

"No matter," Miss Joyce sighed. "When my mother and father arrive, they'll have plenty of good cigarettes for me. Parisiennes, Egyptians, Marylands, long Virginias."

Mrs. Leary smiled weakly in reply.

With her one big agile hand, and the help of her still bondaged other hand, Miss Joyce opened the cigarette packet and quickly waved a Woodbine at the nursing sister in order to hurry the striking of the flint. Perspiration gathered at the bottom of her shoes, soaking her stockings as the sister struck the match.

"Good girl," pronounced Mrs. Leary affectionately, as Miss Joyce drew in the smoke with enormous pleasure. She picked up the copybook and pencil stub as Miss Joyce smoked greedily. She opened to the first page and read Miss Joyce's almost undecipherable, cobweb scrawl, which she knew so well.

Her forehead was creased when she finished reading, not sure if she should correct the mistakes.

Childish nonsense and opera weren't Mrs. Leary's cup of tea. It was 1956 and she was saving to rent one of those new radiograms. However, like a butterfly that dazzles as it flits by, alights for admiration, then, about to be caught, escapes, the exotic words in Lucia's essay did the same to her. It was beyond her but she sensed that a butterfly flapped amidst the letters and between the words. To speak in a foreign language . . . how enthralling and wise, how tongue-twisting, thought Mrs. Leary. She rolled up the copybook and thrust it deep into the pocket of her blue uniform.

It had been she on that winter day five years earlier who

had been sent to Ruislip Airfield one hour by bus from London, all alone to meet a European Airways airplane that had flown the whole way over from France. She had wished on the way down that Dr. Healy had come himself. She hadn't told the doctor that she had never been out of County Clare before except once, for the hurling matches in Dublin, which had turned into a drizzling cold day of being mostly lost and turned around.

She had arrived three hours early, to be sure, and had sat in the waiting terminal listening for the echoey announcement and watching the airplanes and the British people. Neither had she ever seen this close. Her first view of Miss Lucia Joyce had been her straight back, then her wild, irrepressible ginger-colored hair. She stood ramrod straight beside a solidly built French nursing sister on the airfield. Right away Mrs. Leary had sensed something special about Miss Joyce, some buried treasure behind her always darting eyes.

Mrs. Leary overcame her timidity long enough to present herself to the sister, and take a long drink from the features of the patient. She surmised her to be about age forty, a forehead like a brass plate, lots of hair, mismatched bright blue eyes, which made frantic saccadic movements, and a general anxious air of akathisia. All this not unusual for a mental patient being transferred from hospital to hospital after many years in one place. And by airplane across the sea! Who wouldn't be a wreck! I would have had to be put to sleep, she thought to herself. The very thought of flying up in the air made her brittle with nausea. What courage Miss Joyce had, to have flown through the air!

The French sister hurried them both off the airfield and into the terminal. Miss Joyce clawed at the French nurse and said, "Qui ira chercher le charbon si je ne suis pas pour la faire?"

The sister mumbled under her breath what sounded like a saint's name. Miss Joyce's agitation increased. It seemed that what she wanted was a cigarette, which the sister doled out to her from a packet of American cigarettes called Lucky Strikes. Immediately the agitation cooled. The sister lit the cigarette for her with a match from a box in the pocket of her starched habit. Mrs. Leary longed to taste a Lucky Strike, too, but didn't dare ask.

All three went by train, then boat, then motorcar to Barnaderg Bay, Miss Joyce a lamb, in a state of detachment, smoking the whole way.

Mrs. Leary felt that Miss Joyce hadn't noticed her at all on the trip. But when, two days after her admission to a private room on the second floor, St. Lucille's Ward, Mrs. Leary, the ward sister at the time, had looked in on her, she was in restraints. She found Miss Joyce attached to her bed because she had broken two windows and had kicked a full mopping bucket across a corridor. Miss Joyce greeted her like a long-lost friend. "Sister," she exclaimed, "I like your hair. Do mine like yours, like sisters."

Mrs. Leary realized that they could actually be sisters, though she was younger than Miss Joyce by perhaps five years. They seemed to be cut out of the same fabric—big, red-haired, with regal bearings that hid butterfly stomachs.

Mrs. Leary was informed by the matron that Miss Joyce was the daughter of an infamous Irish writer, considered by some to be a great genius, by others and the Church to be a dirty, godless writer banned forevermore in Ireland. Mrs. Leary didn't know which, as her view on reading books was that it was something that ceased after school years finished. She wouldn't dream of reading a book on the Index if she should read one at all. In her spare time she preferred to play cards, mend, and drink gallons of tea.

The staff had been ordered to keep Miss Joyce's identity private so that she would not incur hostility from the other patients and staff. Mrs. Leary pitied Miss Joyce because her godless parents had deprived her of the comforts of Jesus Christ Our Lord.

Occasionally Mrs. Leary would offer a Sweet Afton or Gold Flake cigarette to Miss Joyce, which made her very popular indeed. Also she'd offer samples from tins of biscuits when they could be had, which was rare during those postwar years. Miss Joyce spoke often of a pending visit from her beloved brother, who lived abroad, Mrs. Leary didn't know where.

Miss Joyce would say, "Sister, help me to dress up. Giorgio is coming!" and Mrs. Leary would carefully comb her thick and wild hair. Despite her gentleness, tears of pain always sprang to Miss Joyce's eyes whenever her hair was combed. Then Mrs. Leary would subdue her hair with a ribbon or a slide as she was not permitted pins or combs. An orderly needed always to be in attendance.

The brother never came.

And one morning, while making notations on her chart, Mrs. Leary saw that Mr. James Joyce, the notorious writer, was dead, and Mrs. Nora Joyce, the mother, and Giorgio Joyce, the brother, were still alive, in Switzerland, but had not seen Lucia since the 1930s when they all lived together in Paris.

Miss Joyce rarely spoke about her mother or her father; only about her brother.

One day, though, she talked nonstop about her mother. "My mother worshiped clothes and hats, you know. She was afraid of mice. She didn't like *Madama Butterfly!* Her soul didn't sway with languor and longing to suit Father. She wrote a laundry list on the back of Father's work. She called us good-for-nothings and she was right."

Late in the day the hospital was informed of the mother's death. Miss Weaver, the elderly, pencil-thin family friend, the father's literary executor, who had also been appointed as guardian under the Court of Protection for Lucia, arrived in order to inform Miss Joyce of her mother's death.

When Mrs. Leary escorted two orderlies and Miss Weaver into Miss Joyce's room, Miss Joyce was looking out the meshed window at the chapel and up the circular drive, as she always did with an air of anticipation. Out of the blue she asked Miss Weaver, "Has Mother sent you to bring me a fur coat? Is my mother coming to get me?"

Mrs. Leary felt a chill go up her back. Was she clairvoyant?

"Sit down, Lucia," quietly requested Miss Weaver. Miss Joyce did so, on the bed as there was nowhere else to sit in the room, which was empty of objects or furnishings.

Mrs. Leary politely looked down at the floor.

"Your dear mother died yesterday. I know you were always in her thoughts."

Miss Joyce looked at Sister for confirmation, which came in the form of Mrs. Leary's taking her upper lip into her teeth, biting, tears filling her eyes, while she slowly nodded.

Mrs. Leary cried openly. The death of any mother made her cry. Miss Joyce did not cry at all, only asked Miss Weaver, "I would like her portrait. The portrait done in Lausanne."

Miss Weaver tentatively put her hand on Miss Joyce's cheek. "Yes, my dear, of course."

Miss Joyce repeated her request, "Moi, je voudrais son portrait qu'on a fait à Lausanne."

"Oui," replied Miss Weaver.

Then again she repeated it, "Vorrei il ritratto che è stato fatto a Lausanne."

Miss Weaver did not reply.

Shortly afterward, Miss Joyce went into a two-year eclipse of mayhem and violence mostly against herself. She spent most of these years restrained and in total isolation, experiencing extreme self-loathing and bouts of self-abuse.

Several times during these years Mrs. Leary tried to take her to the church services in the village, and would ask her if she would let the priest come to speak with her. Miss Joyce's only reply to these suggestions was to spit. Mrs. Leary knew in her heart that the Church would help ease her great conflict and suffering. By the time this long episode had begun to subside, Miss Joyce's bright red hair was veined with white.

Miss Joyce was usually not permitted the use of either a pen or pencil. As her charge nurse, Sister Leary enjoyed a special relationship with the patient. She allowed herself to be bullied, sometimes cursed, sometimes cuddled, though even Mrs. Leary, despite her special affection for Lucia (as she had begun to call her, though not by invitation as Miss Joyce rarely asked to be called by her first name), exercised extreme caution when Miss Joyce allowed herself to be touched.

Danger lurked just below the surface at all times. Lucia was capable of enormous violence and had the strength of three men during these interludes. In bright red, the words "COMBATIVE!!! WATCH OUT!!!!" were written across the front of her chart. Mrs. Leary had, in fact, bent a rule by allowing Miss Joyce the pencil stub and the copybook. She had done it as a favor to saintly Miss Weaver and Miss Hutchins, some kind of writer, who had accompanied Miss Weaver on her last visit to Miss Joyce.

Miss Hutchins had presented Mrs. Leary with a carton of Players and a bottle of John Jameson whiskey; both too dear ever to dream of on a nurse's salary. Miss Hutchins had requested, ". . . for the sake of history," which it

appeared she was writing in relation to Miss Joyce's famous father, J. Joyce. She asked that Mrs. Leary encour-
age, and if necessary assist, Miss Joyce in writing down
memories of her early years—about her father and his
work, and, of course, in afterthought, about herself. The
words "for the sake of history" made Mrs. Leary's stomach flutter.

By just that swift glance, Mrs. Leary feared that what
had been written, the fanciful opera, was pure gibberish,
unlikely to be of any use to a real writer like Miss Hutchins. She dreaded Miss Hutchins's return visit, feeling as
though it were she, and not Miss Joyce, who had failed.
To her the words were beautiful and suggested hidden
treasure but, as Miss Hutchins probably hadn't any special affection for the mentally ill, she doubted that Miss
Hutchins would see the writing as anything worthwhile
and praiseworthy.

Impatiently Miss Joyce demanded that a match be
struck for her second Woodbine. "Light, Sister!"

"I am, dearie," Mrs. Leary replied, striking the flint and
waving the flame in front of her ruddy face.

If she let them, Miss Leary knew, her patients would
smoke each and every one of the precious cigarettes.

Mrs. Leary noticed, across the solarium near the altar
to the Virgin, that Mrs. Angeles had snapped out of her
doze and was now bending over, pulling the skin on her
leg. Near to her, but oblivious of her, Miss Ogi menac-
ingly approached, goose-stepping and saluting, her tongue
sticking out of the corner of her mouth.

Sister gave each of them one of her precious Woodbines. If she had enough cigarettes she could keep all three relatively calm, at least until the approaching end of her shift. What happened after that she never knew. They could all hang like monkeys from the rafters when her shift ended for all she knew. Not that she was uncaring, on the contrary, but when she walked through the stone gates with her bicycle all thought of life in Barnaderg Bay vanished from her mind and thoughts of her chores at home replaced them.

When Miss Weaver came for her usual semiannual visit in December, again with Miss Hutchins, Nurse Leary met them in the visitor room, and presented Miss Weaver the opera, in a clean envelope as she had recopied the almost illegible original. She had corrected what she knew was wrong and recopied it on her best cream-colored writing paper with the satin finish.

Miss Hutchins spoke in a nasal, upper-crusty way, which Mrs. Leary could barely understand. She couldn't contain herself and read through the writing without taking a breath or unsticking her lips. Her face seemed to drain of blood, beginning at the tip of her sharp, chalky nose.

Stupefaction froze across her face. *"Tannhäuser* never, *I Puritani* maybe!" she announced to Miss Weaver, and rudely, Mrs. Leary thought, brushed past Mrs. Leary back outside to wait in the taxi. She did not go in to see Miss Joyce. Miss Weaver found it unnecessary to explain, as Miss Joyce had forgotten that Miss Hutchins was supposed to come too for a visit.

II

Pueritia, Adulescentia

Lucia Joyce
Und Der Sängerkrieg
Von Den Kindern

by Lucia Joyce

THIS IS AN OPERA in three acts by Lucia Joyce with libretto in Italian, German, and bits of French based on my childhood years.

LUCIA	*Soprano*
PAPA	*Tenor*
MAMA	*Mezzo-soprano*
NYMPHS, BACCHANTE,	*Sopranos and Bass*
SIRENS, NAIAD	
MINNESINGER	*Baritone*
FOUS LUCIDES	*Tenor*

Time	*Twentieth Century*
Place	*Trieste, Zürich, Paris*

First performance at
BARNADERG BAY HOSPITAL, COUNTY
CLARE, IRELAND, 1956.

Overture

IN THE DISTANCE and behind a gauze curtain, Siren and Nymphs chant. Clarinets, bassoons, horns, are then heard as Beatrice, nine years old, enters. The great Dante sitting up in bed grows a lump in his throat at the sight of her. An electric spark flies between them. Song heard: "Guard'u mare com'e bello," as a Minnesinger brings an unborn-calf glove into Dante's bed. Dante is naked. The sound of a clarinet. The glove belongs to Bacchante. The Minnesinger covers his coglioni and his hatrack with the baby-soft glove.

The scene changes: A small Irish boy of seven says, "Bloody." He receives four pandies on his tender palm, held open in front of him and given by a red-cheeked Christian Brother. The third and fourth pandies leave welts. The boy's mother enters and pushes his head into the toilet bowl, then she flushes for saying the word "Prick."

Against the sky, a goose-step of lightning, as mad nuns in the nearby madhouse shriek. (Scene can be with or without thunderclaps.) The boy is kneeling, his eyes are weak. He prays to the Blessed Virgin Mary for love sacred. He turns and sees a headstone chiseled "J. Joyce." He turns again. Peagreen bile runs from his mother's mouth. He listens to music. He dreams of love profane coming someday to take him far away as the sound of a lone clarinet against quivering strings is heard.

Act I

THE ACT opens to trills of violins as the gauze curtain rises on the city of Trieste. Yellow spotlight skulks along the wall of a rented room. Three photographic copies of Ivan Meštrović sculptures are held on by pins above a tousled bed. The first print, on the left, a pregnant peasant woman writhing in pain, the pain of giving birth. In the center, a skeletal child sucking at the almost deflated breast of its mother. On the right, a naked woman, very old, ugly as sin.

Crashing of cymbals. Piccolos and oboes melt in. Lights go up as Papa and Mama hold a creamy baby, the baby born in the paupers' ward on St. Anne's Day. Papa removes the baby's white fur undershirt and kisses, suckles the baby's chalk-white shoulder blade. Mama then takes off the baby's little white cotton slippers and kisses first one then two of baby's small spongy soles of feet. Lucia, the baby, is naked in a soapy porcelain washbowl. Mama and Papa, Adam and Eve, also naked together suds and tickle the baby. Laughter from them and from voices offstage.

Mama puts her large breast into the baby's mouth. Lucia sucks it in and in. It jumps out with popping noise and with spittle left on the skin. Mama puts it back and laughs. Papa kisses Mama as Papa's hatrack grows into an ashplant which taps its head on the washbowl. Its head grows into a bronze cobra, thumping against the wash-bowl and so forceful that it lifts the washbowl and baby up into the air to the parents' eye level. Lucia holds on to the breast with her mouth. The breast is an ivory elephant tusk. Lucia's two hands pat the sides of the warm breast.

The baby's body is wet from the bath. The parents lick the baby as wild beasts do their young. The baby jiggles her little plump legs in the air, kicking the air. Faintly, a song of sirens as Papa sings "Dir tone Lob." The lights come up on the Piazza Giambattista Vico where groups of Croats, Greeks, Italians, Jews, and Austrians in the street listen to the beautiful melodious tenor voice of Papa coming from the window above them. His voice an invocation. One by one Austrians and Italians drop to their knees in prayer to the Virgin Mary. A somber hymn is heard as the lights lower.

Return to setting of Scene One. The light comes up. Lucia cries in her parents' big bed. Pulling the neck of her nightdress away Lucia reveals red and angry boils ringing her neck. Papa is in the small bed, suffering from rheumatic fever, also painful iritis. They eat pasta for Christmas dinner. Mama's voice is mocking as she serves them their food. Mama also takes in washing and ironing. Mama talks about clothes and hats. Shouts are heard from the street below. "Ubbriacone!" Mama soaks bread in milk and wraps it in a handkerchief with a monogram. She ties the poultice around Lucia's neck. Papa sings as darkness comes. "One little girl, one little apple tree."

In the darkness a chant of Pilgrims is heard. The light comes up. There are leeches around Papa's eyes. Duet is sung: "Die Meistersinger." Papa and Mama are riding on a train. They see a Greek. This bodes good luck. They see a Jew. He exudes sex. In the public lavatory, a ring falls off Papa's finger and into the lavatory. Mama and Papa try to get it out.

New scene: Papa wakes and plays the piano.

Three children come for English lessons from Papa. These children come naked, they are thirteen years old, all girls. Papa gets red spots on his cheeks, he makes the girls cover themselves with blankets. But they only cover their heads and shoulders. Their exposed hairless little plump heinies are painted patent-leather black. The girls hold Papa around his bony thigh as they try to hide from each other. It's a game. Mama spanks them all as Lucia looks on.

A pause, then Papa throws a manuscript into the fire. Mama pulls it out though the edges are burned. A review falls to ground: In block letters the words: *Cloacal Obsessions*. Papa steps forward and announces, "Puzza di sesso. Tannhäuser." Jews, Greeks, Serbs, Somarians, Austrians, Italians, gather below in the street listening to Papa sing a lullaby. "C'era una volta, una bella bambina." A pause, then the sound of hunting horns as soldiers arrive on the street. The sun shines down. The sea sparkles. Father sings with so much feeling that the clavichord almost can't be heard.

Act II

IN DARKNESS is heard "Pourquoi me reveiller . . ."

The act opens on Mama sitting in the sunshine in front

of St. Antoniuskirche, Zürich, she is weeping. Stage left, Papa pulls an unwilling Lucia, seven years old, along the Mühlebachstrasse to school. In Zürich Lucia must speak Zürichdeutsch. The bells of Fraumünster ring out, Sech-selaüten, end of winter. Later, Lucia, Mama, and Papa walk around the lake. Mama throws a paper into the gutter and a Swiss policeman blows his whistle. He stops Mama demanding, "Das aufheben!"

New scene opens as Papa writes a book in the hotel room using a green suitcase as a desk. Propped up in bed fully clothed, eating chocolates, Mama reads pornography out loud to Papa. She reads from Paul de Kock, from John Cleland. In the background Lucia gets piano lessons but listens to Mama read.

At the end of the day, Papa plays on his guitar. "Addio! Del passato" from *La Traviata*. Then Mama plays on the piano "Parigi, O Cara." The light has almost gone and Papa sings, "Un bel dì, vedremo" to Mama but Mama isn't moved enough to suit him. Lucia is blindfolded. The sound of a cat lapping milk is heard over a loudspeaker all across Zürich.

New scene: Lucia, age ten, lies on a small cot in a darkened hotel room. Mama and Papa are in a larger bed together in the same room. The curtain blows into the room. Outside the window snow falls steadily, past the yellow glow of a street lamp. Papa speaks quietly to Lucia in Italian. He speaks liltingly to Mama in Italian. Mama replies to him in English. Mama and Papa sleep head to foot in bed. Silence surrounds them. Mama gets out of bed, the springs squeak, she walks to the toilet. She wears a loose nightgown. Her big breasts swing as she walks. The sound of splashing urination fills the room. Papa shifts in bed. Lucia is afraid she will piss too.

New scene: Lucia winds up a mahogany gramophone at a resort hotel on Lago Maggiore. Next to her Mama reads pornography just under her breath. Lucia and Mama climb into a small boat on Lago Maggiore, they row into the center of the lake. Just then a dramatic thunderstorm comes. Clashes of thunder and lightning engender terrible fright in Mama.

Later, in Zürich, Papa holds Lucia above the crowd to watch the Sechselaüten, end of winter. Papa's eyes, gray owl eyes, are the eyes of Athena. Papa's book sells only 450 copies. Papa goes to see *La Traviata*. Humming tunes, the family walks together along the Seefeldstrasse, the Universitätstrasse, the Kreuzstrasse, the Reinhardstrasse.

Reprise: Lucia getting piano lesson. The teacher stands behind her. Lucia feels his mushy hatrack against her spine. Father has Greek friends. He has Jewish friends. Lucia sees a Jewish woman combing her dark hair, she has soft, sleepy eyes. Papa teaches a Jewish student. Papa points out a bronze statue of a Jewish woman lounging in an armchair stroking a cat. Papa slits open a letter, money pours out of the envelope for him. It comes from women, women with no names, no faces. Mama dances the jig. Men on the street look at Mama's heaving chest. Naked, husky Jewish men stand in a group. Mama walks with a straight back. She smells of fresh sweat.

High above her, stage right, Papa stands with his back to a window smoking a long cheroot. He has on a chiffon burgundy dressing gown, carpet slippers are on his feet.

His left hand is deep in the pocket of his dressing gown. Papa's fascination is for Lucia, he's always watching her, always making notes. He has grown a goat's beard. Fous Lucides chant and the curtain drops.

Act III

CURTAIN RISES. Paris, the Gare de Lyon. Lights come up on a small hotel room where Papa, with blanket wrapped around shoulders, writes on a green suitcase. Lucia gets singing lessons. When Papa exits Lucia looks into Papa's green suitcase and sees glass, pebbles, matchsticks, bits of paper. Papa returns to the stage and drinks a glass of buttermilk.

New Year's Eve: Naiad throws a loaf of bread against the hotel-room door. Papa speaking Italian, Mama loses her temper, belittles, mocks. Mama and Papa speak Italian to each other then Mama slaps Lucia. Papa turns away and sings Purcell. Lucia drops a piece of china. Mama calls her "butterfingers." Papa gives her a geranium from a potted plant. Papa smiles at her then puts his hand in front of his mouth to hide his teeth.

The scene changes: Mama and Papa and Lucia, age thirteen, are together in the theatre seeing La Fille de Madame Angot in French, it's a light operetta. Then they stroll to a café. It's afternoon. Papa drinks lime-blossom tea, Mama drinks China black tea, Lucia drinks Hervain tea.

Back at the small hotel room: Lucia with fever and rash in a small cot set up at the foot of her parents' bed. She hides her sprouting breasts with a sheet. There's a print of Vermeer, a drawing of Delft on the wall. In the street below a yellow spotlight reveals Mama sitting in a small booth in a phonograph shop listening to opera music. Languorous, her fingertips rub her tongue. The spotlight is extinguished. Across the room from Lucia, Papa's black wood Irish cane with large knobby top stands upright between his knees as he sprawls in a chair. He wears flannel trousers, dirty tennis shoes. He stares into space with a look of distraction. Papa is frozen. Papa's eyes are covered with dark glasses. Mama returns and threatens, "I will take Lucia home to Ireland if you drink again."

Night has come. Paris, the city of lights. A lone star shines down from the sky, brightly shining. Paris is aswim with gaiety, artists, fashionable clothes, Americans, Russians, homosexuals also abound. The siren strums an Irish harp. Papa sings, "O Du mein holder Abendstern."

Fame comes.

New scene: Lucia is sixteen, she has grown a woman's body. She takes dancing lessons with many different teachers: a Swede, a Swiss, a Hungarian, an American, a Russian. She spends eight hours a day dancing. Papa is attacked by a dog. His glasses break. Papa is then attacked and ridiculed by critics shouting: "Sham masterpiece," "Pornography," "Banned in Ireland," "Meditation on garbage." Also heard, "Masterpiece."

Leeches are around Papa's eyes. He quarrels with friends. He receives injections of cocaine in his eye. Also injections of arsenic, injections of phosphorus. Seventeen teeth are extracted. He has no teeth from April until June in the Paris chill. He has a nervous collapse and goes for a rest to a *maison de santé*. The window to his soul is broken by a rock.

Lucia practices her dancing. Cellos are joined by bassoons and oboes, yearning cries crisscrossed between strings and woodwinds. Lucia's curling reddish thick hair is flung as she dances. It's crisp with electricity, shining. Papa reclines on the couch. He is whispering into Mama's ear. He whispers the secret of the new book. Lucia is taught the secret of "Prelude to Tristan and Isolde" on the piano. A black cat sits on the piano. Papa stretches out in bed, a patch over his eye. Lucia plays the piano for Papa. Mama reads from the *Encyclopaedia Britannica* to Papa. Mama's large portrait is on the wall. Papa polishes his double-lens dark glasses with a silk handkerchief.

New scene: Papa, Mama, and Lucia are on holiday. They sleep three to a room. There are feral sleep odors each night in Salzburg, Munich, Nice, Strasbourg, Frankfurt, Le Havre, Antwerp, Ghent, Brussels, Waterloo. They buy cameos from an old Italian crone standing on a bridge between France and Italy. Papa mounts the cameos onto rings.

Papa is in a hospital bed. Mama sleeps beside him.

Mama is in a hospital bed. Papa sleeps beside her. They are inseparable. Only Mama knows the secret of Papa's new book for sixteen years. Lucia asks what the secret is but Mama won't tell her. Papa won't tell her either. Lucia is too stupid to guess, is a terrible disappointment.

Scene changes: Lucia is alone at camp in Normandy.
Lucia has been given the sheet music of Brahms's *Lieder*.
Instead she plays "Prelude to Tristan and Isolde." Her
playing is followed by ecstatic songs for cellos.

Lucia tries drawing lessons. Greek flags adorn the vesti-
bule. Lucia wants to ride upon hatracks coiled, hatracks
ballooning, hatracks dripping hot olive oil, wants mushy
hatracks against her face, her belly, wants a hatrack in each
hand, wants to look into the squinting eye at the tip of a
tall hatrack.

Papa makes vocalizzi, accompanying himself on the
piano. Mama returns to the flat, her thick hair is shingled.
Supplicants encircle and oil Papa as he reclines on the
couch. With spider legs Papa sings "Oh the brown and the
yellow ale!" He sings with rolled *r*'s, his eyelids are closed.
"Confuse the professors for three hundred years," Papa
predicts. He writes on large cards in colored pencils. He
can't read or see to write. All must help him.

Lucia confesses all bodily deformities. Mama makes
compresses for Papa's eyes with a bucket of ice water. All
three have supper at the Café de la Paix. "Nora read my
books; Nora read my books," Papa begs.

Scene: Lucia, eighteen years old, celebrates at Grand
Hôtel des Bains et de Londres Fécamp. Afterward, Papa
takes to his bed. He is afflicted with insomnia. Papa hal-
lucinates, has nightmares, studies Lucia like a specimen.
Children in faraway Tibet and Somaliland find the name
of their nearby rivers in Papa's work. They love Papa who
speaks the Triestine dialect to Mama, and to Lucia. Papa's

disciples fill the room with other languages. Papa's work is everywhere in the flat.

Lucia's sin of strabismus, sin of scar, take all her thought and time. Because of them Lucia cannot brush her thick reddish hair, she cannot iron or wash her clothes. She cannot keep Mama from saying that she's leaving Papa, keep Papa from drinking too much wine. She cannot control growing agitation, one more surgery on Papa's eyes.

Her chair keeps rocking after she gets up.

Insects cover Lucia's skin. Lucia's big toes are tied together to keep men from looking between her legs. Papa strums on the harp. The light fades.

Forgiveness only when Papa's ashplant would sprout leaves.

Minnesingers and Fous Lucides arrive to tell the miracle. Tannhäuser's hatrack has sprouted leaves but it's too late for Lucia Joyce.

A funeral procession carrying the bier of Lucia Joyce passes in the street below and the light is extinguished.

The curtain rapidly falls.

At Fifty

N 1957 the recently developed antipsychotic drug chlorpromazine (Thorazine) arrived at Barnaderg Bay. Although it caused a small mustache to grow across Miss Joyce's upper lip, the medication lessened her violent outbursts. Periods of increased lucidity began and her hushed-up identity became common knowledge as she now announced herself to one and all as Miss Lucia Joyce, daughter of Nora and James Joyce, who had traveled to Ireland, Plyme, Italy, Switzerland, France, England, Austria, and Holland. "James Augustine Aloysius Joyce and Nora Joseph Barnacle Joyce. *Those* Joyces," she would announce if the names were confused, as Joyce was such a common name in Ireland.

In 1958 when Miss Weaver visited, Lucia welcomed her with unusual affection. Lucia was allowed to take her for a walk on the

hospital grounds, and presented her with a red felt dachs-
hund, which she had made during occupational therapy.

"Mind your step, Miss Weaver," suggested Lucia as
the visit was drawing to a close. Miss Weaver looked
down at the ground. Lucia shook her head. "Not now,
next November," she instructed.

Miss Weaver smiled indulgently, but the following November when she tripped outside her room and fell onto
the floor on her left side, the first thing that entered her
mind after the first wave of pain had passed was Lucia's
face.

Lucia was now permitted crude writing implements.
Mrs. Leary or a nurse in training often supervised Miss
Joyce's new letter-writing frenzy. Gratuities and gifts arrived regularly from Miss Weaver with requests that Miss
Joyce receive as much personal attention as Mrs. Leary
could give. Miss Joyce's letter-writing binges were accom-
plished using small pencil stubs, as pens were still considered too dangerous.

Miss Joyce began to barrage people far and wide with
letters. She wrote to Queen Elizabeth, Charles de Gaulle,
Sir Winston Churchill, as well as her brother in Zürich; to
a former piano teacher in Trieste; to an Uncle Stanni,
whom she had secretly called "Deasil," also in Trieste; to
an Uncle Charles in America; to Miss Weaver, her legal
guardian; to her father's English, French, German, American, Italian publishers.

Not seeming to recall the fact of their demise, she also
often wrote to her mother and father. Sometimes she
wrote separately to her parents, and sometimes together.

She wrote to them in Paris, Trieste, and one time to a place called Plyme in a country called Rhoda, which needed an airmail stamp, Miss Joyce said, but neither the place nor the country was familiar to Sister Leary or the postmistress.

Considering her letter writing a good outlet, the doctor and matron encouraged her. Sister Leary often sat and crocheted doilies for Christmas gifts during what should have been her tea break while Lucia composed these letters. Because in those years international exchanges were not stabilized, Lucia's limited pocket money would not go far. She had a liking for French and American cigarettes, and rarely could she even afford Sweet Aftons, the best of the Irish, let alone both cigarettes and postage stamps for her letters. Always helpful, Sister Leary often provided a stamp or two, a cigarette or two. After an afternoon of letter writing, Sister Leary would gather up the letters, stack them, and tuck them away in the deep pockets of her uniform.

Later at home, when evening tea was set out for Jim and before the children had arrived home, she would take Miss Joyce's stack of letters and separate them into piles—real people (the lawyer, the brother) famous people (Winston Churchill), dead people (parents, her father's long-dead mother, her mother's mother), imaginary people (one M. Osiris). Then she would recopy the real people and famous people, stamp them, if her own budget allowed, and laid them out for the postman. The remaining letters she'd gather up to discard but because of those remembered words "for the sake of history" was not able to. Instead she kept them in an old Black Magic chocolate tin.

When they overflowed the chocolate tin, she tied twine around the bundle and found a larger tin, this one from biscuits. She kept it beneath her hot-water bottles, medicine, and soap lifted from the hospital, in the linen cupboard beside the four love letters Jim had written to her when he had been back in Cookstown, County Tyrone, for his mother's funeral when they had already been married two years. His erotic longing for her was so intense that she would have died if another living soul had ever laid eyes on those letters. She tied a small jingle bell to the twine so that she could hear if they were ever disturbed.

Replies came to Lucia's letters, small gifts as well. Because several letters had been exchanged with some of her former beaux, Lucia decided that she must choose a husband from among those who remained living in her memory, or who had returned letters to her. Lucia had not seen any of these men since 1935 or before, but it hadn't occurred to her that any one of them had changed in the slightest or that the war had interrupted or redirected all their lives.

"I must marry one of them!" she told Mrs. Leary.

"Why must you marry at all?" asked the nurse.

"My mother loves nothing more than a wedding. I do as well. Mind you, no wedding ring, no chains of slavery!"

"Are you in love, Lucia?" asked Mrs. Leary.

"Yes. My true love, but he was lost in the war. He was a Jew. He came to get me during the thunder and bombing but they arrested him. He was yeast."

Sister had never seen or met a Jew.

Lucia added, "He was also a Greek. He was illiterate but he could recite poems by heart. A Greek wrote a book which proved that Athens is the gravitational center of the world. Do you know that? My father told me, and he was never wrong. My father had a theory that the *Odyssey* is a Semitic poem. Can you swallow that? That's quite a fish."

Sister had never seen or met a Greek either. "But you must not marry a man that you do not love," she instructed.

"I must not marry a man *you* love," Lucia commented with irony. "I will not marry Mr. Leary."

If she only knew how rudely Mr. Leary spoke of her patients at the hospital, she would not be so kind about him. "I dreamed of letters in a chocolate tin," Lucia announced to Mrs. Leary, squinting her mismatched eyes up at her.

How could she know? wondered Mrs. Leary. Can she see through walls? "Flies are buzzing around the letters." Her left eye locked with Mrs. Leary's right eye. Mrs. Leary felt as if she was being x-rayed.

Lucia unlocked her eye. "I must marry, Sister. Mother will never rest unless I do. She loves weddings, love letters in a tin or not."

Nurse Leary's face burned. She longed to change the subject away from letters and tins. She noticed a burn between Lucia's long fingers. As she dressed the burn she told her, "You must tell me when you've a burn like this, it could become infected."

Lucia looked at the injury with no interest. "I watched

another girl wearing my clothes do that to herself. She gets a bigger allowance than I do and gets to have more cigarettes than I do. Do you know if my brother gets a bigger allowance than I do?"

Sister said that she did not know, finding it too discouraging to tell her again that she had no news of Giorgio. She wanted to avoid a reaction such as she had got once when she had reminded Lucia that both her father and mother were dead and buried.

"Under the earth?" Lucia had asked.

"Where else," had been her reply.

"There's a rat stuck in my throat." Lucia had gripped her own throat until it had turned crimson. When finally the seizure had passed, Lucia again asked, "Are they under the earth?"

Nurse looked the other way, down at the nail scissors she had brought and been unable to use because Lucia could not stand to be touched by human hands that day, that week. Lucia didn't wait for an answer. She spoke up curtly, "That's what they'd like us to believe. They've gone to the opera. Father has on his grandfather's waistcoat with the hunting scenes and little dogs' faces, Mother has on a new fur coat, Father has got leeches around his eyes. If they fall they wiggle and jerk and can't be caught. They couldn't eat boiled leg of mutton or turnips and cabbage again under the earth. See how impossible it is! Who else will take nine days to prepare the plum pudding, then carry it grandly to the table in its very large service dish if they are underground? They are fooling you but they're not fooling me. They are sly. They study me like a specimen night and day. Tell them to get up and quit the farce. They must just shake off the dirt and stand up, stop singing "*Addio terra, addio cielo.*"

Needless to say Mrs. Leary would not again say that there was no indication that the brother was coming to see her, nor would she mention that both parents had died. She stared hard at her wedding ring.

"Is Dr. Healy sexy? I can see that his hands are hot and tremble sometimes." Lucia declared, watching fire ignite on sister's cheeks, liking to tease her with subjects that Mrs. Leary considered unmentionable.

"Won't you let me cut your nails, Miss Joyce? They're beginning to curl over," Mrs. Leary begged, avoiding the question that had made her cheeks feel hot, as she had always felt a tingling ache between her legs when the doctor walked by.

Once again, as usual, the nail cutting was refused.

The new medication also decreased Lucia's extreme suspiciousness. She continued nonetheless to insist to her doctors that her veins and arteries were made of glass piping.

When Lucia began her letter-writing barrage, she entreated far and near to assist her departure from Barnaderg Bay. She met with great frustration.

Because she was no longer violent there was no reason for her not to be able to live outside the stultification of hospital walls. She blissfully related to Mrs. Leary her fantasy of going back out into the world.

"I imagine myself in a small house. I imagine putting on a delicious afternoon tea with cakes and sandwiches and real thick cream. I imagine a silver letter opener on a mahogany desk, hairpins. I imagine carefully combing a little girl's hair, making a braid down her back that touches her heels. I have not seen or touched a child up close since 1935, Sister, can you imagine that? Now that I am grown-up I can keep doves and songbirds, sleep until noon again, and go to a funeral, which my mother never allowed me to do before."

Regardless of the doors that did not open and the letters that did not come, she was convinced, daily, that her beloved brother would arrive and effect this liberation for her.

She remained unflinchingly convinced of this always.

Miss Weaver, though very, very old, was allowed to take Miss Joyce for a walk when she visited but not in the rain. If it rained they would sit side by side in the solarium. On one of these rainy days Miss Weaver sat beside her on the saggy horsehair couch and presented Lucia with a box wrapped in tissue paper and tied with a gray ribbon. Lucia became very excited, then held her breath as she undid the paper. She nodded when she saw a box filled with watercolor paints and brushes; a drawing block was part of the surprise.

A nurse's aide brought a tin with water for Lucia, and Lucia started immediately to sketch out a drawing. Miss Weaver, worn-out from the tiresome journey, made no effort at conversation. After all she had known and taken an interest in Lucia for over forty years. They knew each other very, very well. "Did you love Dr. Macdonald," Lucia suddenly inquired. "Or perhaps did he love you?"

Undaunted, Miss Weaver shook her head and smiled peacefully.

Lucia biliously continued, "He didn't love me. He gave me fifteen injections of bovine serum himself, and then another ten. Seven weeks. Even a field horse would have struggled, Miss Weaver."

Miss Weaver concurred. "You were a very brave girl. On top of everything it was a terribly hot summer, 1935. Did I fail my friends, Lucia? Did I disappoint you all?" she asked without rancor but with real interest.

"It was I that disappointed everyone, I'm afraid, Miss Weaver," Miss Joyce keened. "I should have married Mr. Fernandez. Mother would have liked that. I had so many marriage proposals I can't even count them. Yva had only three. I should never have stopped dancing, Miss Weaver. That's where it all went wrong, where I began to fall instead of dive."

Lucia concluded her drawing and signed her name, "Lucia Joyce," the year, "1961." Then she wrote "Miss Weaver" at the top of the drawing, which was a good likeness of a kind lady wearing a hat, and handed it to Miss Weaver as a gift. "I was uneasy with you back then, Miss Weaver. You were so distinguished and well dressed, but I'm not afraid of you anymore. Thanks to you Father didn't unlearn English as he threatened."

Miss Weaver died twelve days later.

Lucia suffered a bout of psychosis passionelle, believing that Winston Churchill was in love with her. She felt no ache of love for him—he smoked a smelly cigar and had big, florid cheeks. Olfactory hallucinations overcame her

as well. Her doctor took on the appearance of a red potato. When she looked at a clock she would see arms,
numbers, glass, brass, but not the parts together. The
same went for calendars. She listened closely to chirpings
of birds and to the wind. Both were bringing messages,
divinations, signals, warnings, messages of love.

IV

At Sixty

M R. *ELLMANN*, the biographer, led a parade of biographers and scholars to Barnaderg Bay. They always brought cigarettes as currency, boxes of Cadbury's chocolate from England to Mrs. Leary. Nurse Leary, to all, had become identified as the palm that had to be greased in order to gain access to Miss Joyce. In Mrs. Leary's heart, she was Lucia's protector. Most of St. Lucille's Ward called Lucia "Nurse Leary's pet."

An elderly professor, Mr. Carr, approached Mrs. Leary. Could he speak with Miss Joyce? He enclosed a letter from the solicitor for her father's estate giving his approval to a series of interviews. Mrs. Leary, though disapproving, didn't refuse this or any of the other requests, which became quite common. In all areas of her life she rarely if ever said the word "no."

Mr. Carr hoped that Miss Joyce might have

some information to impart to him and the world of Joyce scholarship relating to what, if anything, James Joyce was working on or contemplating for future work at the time the Germans occupied France, or earlier. He reminded Lucia that he had twice been in her company in Paris, once for lunch with her former fiancé Samuel Beckett, and even before that, at the home of her father.

"Should I have married Mr. Beckett?" she asked him.

He thought for a long while. "Yes, you should have," he replied sincerely.

"But Mr. Beckett travels. He's too tall. Doesn't he drink?" she asked, and added, making a sour face "Imagine being married to Oblomov!" Then she laughed.

When she stopped laughing she looked off over Mr. Carr's shoulder and added, "Mr. Calder was the best lover, you know, but Albert Hubbell was the first."

Lucia did slightly remember this man, but not with pleasure. She couldn't remember exactly why, but thought it had to do with his politics. She remembered that one time he had agreed to murder beautiful trees—an oak and an ash—for no better reason than that they made a mess. That, then, he had turned against her father who disagreed about destroying trees. Her father had forgiven him for the sake of a long friendship, but one day Carr had walked silently by and had looked away and had not spoken.

Miss Joyce wrote an essay that she titled "The War." Suspicious of Mr. Carr, Mrs. Leary lurked nervously nearby, sensitive to the fact that Miss Joyce did not like Mr. Carr because of his loud and false laugh. She wanted to be in hearing range if Miss Joyce went off her head.

The War

by Lucia Joyce

I TORE my fur coat all to bits because of the war. Because it was coming Miss Weaver slept beside me and held my hand all night. Why dance? Why care when none of us could wake from the nightmare? Mother shook me by my shoulders, I still didn't wake up. Nobody read Papa's book because of the war, it had come to spite him. Papa helped sixteen Jews to escape from Germany: First he played on the piano, the song "Hatikvah," singing to them in Hebrew. I sang to them for courage, "You're the Cream in My Coffee" in four languages—French, Italian, Swiss-German, and English—to cheer these fearful people. Garlic would be the key to their safety. Ireland, North and South America, Switzerland, were places of safety. Father would never dare to set foot on a plane, nor would he agree to save himself and us in Ireland. England either because he called the English a reptile-like race ending with Mr. Carr, a true snake who turned and spat at us after fifteen years a friend. Add this to a brain on fire, a war, a hat on the bed.

All through the war my blood stagnated especially the blood in my head. When the war was ending they drained the blood from my head, two cupfuls spilled out. For the first time since 1928 I washed my hair with my own ten fingers. It is not possible to recover fully the red-colored hair that had been lost in war years. I was once the kind that laughed before you even began to tickle me. I saw things a little girl usually doesn't see. Vision upon vision visited me.

The nurse and doctor say that my parents are dead in the war. But where is proof? Who witnessed their stopped hearts? Perhaps they have emigrated. Irish often emigrate. No one threw themselves on their corpses.

Did the floors and walls and furniture of their hotels shake and tremble around the clock as did mine? I see their faces alive. I never see my children or any children. I have not touched a child since 1935. I see my true love walking toward me through the war but only walking, not arriving.

The war will truly end in 1976. It will have taken forty-eight years from each of us.

———————

"The War" was read by Professor Carr at the 1970 Symposium in Cologne before a crowd of two hundred. Dr. Bernheim, a Joyce scholar from Salt Lake City, Utah, had penned a piece titled "Mela Surejo" to be read as a companion to "The War." Dr. Bernheim argued that it was a sublunary companion to "Giacomo Joyce" but generally "The War" was of little use to Joyce scholarship, which was growing more lively with each passing year.

Nonetheless eight Ph.D. candidates used material from it as a basis for their theses, and three libraries—in London, Texas, and Prague—bid to purchase it for their special collections. When it was discovered that the handwritten copy on cream-colored cheap writing paper was not the original (as Mrs. Leary had again wanted to be helpful, and had recopied Lucia's work in a clear hand onto her best stationery), the price dropped. It was purchased nonetheless by rich Texans.

James Joyce's name was known to all in the hospital. No wonder his child had gone "off her head" people said. Only God knew what depravities she had been made to witness, growing up with a likely sex pervert! Being the daughter of such a dirty-minded writer couldn't have been easy, though no one had read any of his books. He was known to someone there as a man who had written an enormous tome that took place from beginning to end in an outhouse on an Irish country farm.

The closest Barnaderg Bay came to having a real celebrity occurred in 1969 when the sister of the Archbishop of the West of Ireland was brought to St. Lucille's Ward. She believed that Hitler himself had sewn a wireless radio into her cranium and was determined to transfer military information through her to the other spies planted around her in the hospital. Even the splashing sound of her own urine, she believed, was coded with information. She applied great effort to breaking up the natural force and rhythm of her liquid evacuations. She also suffered from echolalia, repeating exactly what she heard being said to her like a very obedient parrot. Her name was Assumpta.

Great attention was paid on alternating Sundays when the Archbishop would drive up in a black car. Even Mrs. Leary, several times, though it was her day off, came to catch a glimpse of the Archbishop. She once brought her five grandchildren but kept them outside the great gate. The Archbishop would offer blessings to those patients and staff that had gathered in his path on the way in, but not on the way out. The staff used his visits as a kind of blackmail to patients keen on being allowed to entreat him for a blessing by lurking in the corridor and stairwell to St. Lucille's.

Lucia Joyce, as her father might have before her, treated the fortnightly visits of the Archbishop with indifference. "Barbarians armed with crucifixes," she would comment.

She would ask to go to her room if she happened to be in the dayroom when the fanfare began. While the Archbishop was present on the premises, a kind of electric current of excitement and agitation crackled along the corridors and through the public rooms. After his departure it was as though the current had been disconnected, the switch thrown off. Many fell right asleep. At this time Lucia would return to the dayroom saying to no one and to everyone, *"Leben Sie wohl!"*

Aunt Kathleen, her mother's sister, and her husband, John, visited her, cousin Delimata, Maria Jolas did too, and Mr. and Mrs. Budgen did as well. She could sometimes walk the grounds with her visitors, have tea, other times there was silence if Lucia was not right.

A nun from Dublin visited once each year usually in October. She brought rosaries and issues of *Catholic News*. Mrs. Leary and the nun put their heads together, hoping to spoonfeed Lucia with a little religion. The *Catholic News* was given away. The rosaries Lucia lowered into a pair of stockings.

Lucia's hospital bills were paid through the law firm representing the Joyce estate, her weekly allowance as

well. The accruing corpus of Miss Joyce's share in her
father's growing estate was kept in a bank in London and
controlled by a firm of solicitors. Miss Joyce was able to
petition the account for extra funds, though, for reasons
never explained, she was not to know the exact pound-for-
pound total of her holdings.

With Mrs. Leary's help she petitioned by letter for a fur
coat. She was refused. She petitioned for a piano. She was
refused. She petitioned for a trip to Germany to see her
brother. She was refused. New Easter and Christmas out-
fits she received. She loved new shoes and the estate was
more than generous. She hated trying them on so chose by
attraction and smell rather than fit. She would caress and
admire rather than wear her new acquisitions. She bought
patent leather for the sheen, Italian leather for the tang. By
arrangement the shoe shop in the village brought samples
of shoes for Miss Joyce to choose from. She petitioned
repeatedly for the estate to expedite her release from Barnaderg Bay. She was neither refused nor encouraged. To
these requests there was only silence.

She sat day after day, year after year, alone by her
window. In the same way as when her mother and father
had taken her in 1913 to watch the needle boats in San
Sabba, just outside of Trieste, she now watched the arriv-
als and departures of generations of sparrows.

Ever newer antipsychotic medication arrived at Barnaderg Bay Hospital, an array of more refined phenothia-
zines. Because of them violence almost had ceased to
erupt. As well as a mustache a small beard grew on Miss
Joyce's face. At first it was ginger and salt, then slowly all

salt—white as new snow, as snowy white as her still un-
ruly and wild hair had become.

The medication also caused Lucia to gain weight; dis-
charge seeped from her breasts. She underwent some
damage to her retina, and endured a constant dry mouth.

By 1967 Sister Leary was allowed to take Lucia, along
with several other patients, to tea in the village. If the
people in the village and in the tearoom knew who the
ladies were, they did not show it.

When Miss Weaver died she was replaced by her god-
daughter, Miss Jane Lidderdale, who visited Lucia three
times a year. Other visitors appeared, among them James
Stephens's daughter; Nelly Joyce, the widow of Uncle
Stanni; David Monro of Monro Pennefather. Lucia Joyce
sometimes confused Mr. Monro and other of the men
with her brother Giorgio, and these visits were occasions
of great joy as well as great misery.

As the date of a visit approached Lucia's hopes rose
that Giorgio was coming to take her "home," wherever
that was. She would live in high anticipation of his visits,
counting the days, hours and minutes (though concepts of
time seemed to swell her brain: Was it a week? How could
it be five years when it was yesterday?). She behaved
badly, causing all who attended to her needs great anxiety
because she was again capable of kicking food trays,
breaking windows.

The men bravely ignored her case of mistaken identity,
and showered devotion and attention on Lucia, as did
Miss Lidderdale and all the ladies who visited, giving in to
her every whim.

So did Nelly Joyce, a favorite of Lucia's, offering fresh

cream on the scones, pack upon pack of precious cigarettes, lots of giggling because they were the same age. The
guests were not aware of her terrible deflation after visits.

Giorgio did visit her one time for one hour in 1967 with
his new wife. Lucia was never sure if it was really him; his
hair was steel gray.

She resumed her waiting, hoping on his next visit she
could tell for sure if it really was Giorgio.

Lucia was not conscious that she had aged in the slightest and never ceased to be curious as to whether or not
Giorgio's allowance had increased to a point that made it
larger than her own.

Sometimes now the hospital took her on outings, or
presented a concert which she would attend. One time, in
fact, Lucia Joyce gave a small concert, a piano recital, and
several ladies from the ward attended. She played for
fifteen minutes and decided that was quite enough Wagner for them for that day.

Although unconscious of aging or fattening, Miss Joyce
became more and more supersensitive to the fact that she
was not married. She spoke of someone who had loved
her always coming to "cleat" to her, but also began to
reconsider some of the "runners-up." She did not want to
die before she had been married, stood before a judge, her
father on one side, her mother on the other, and slept in
a nuptial bed. Did Mrs. Leary think it was too late to
marry Mr. Beckett?

"Yes," Mrs. Leary would reply.

"Sister, have I made a mistake with Alex Ponisovsky,
should I reconsider? What about McGreevy?"

Mrs. Leary didn't have the heart to tell her that Alex

Ponisovsky had died twenty years before, that he had been arrested by the Nazis in April of 1944 and perished inside one of those famous camps. Albert Hubbell was a grandfather. So was Mr. Calder. Mr. Beckett sent her a pretty box of French talcum powder or some other gift, like a subscription to the *Illustrated London News*, for her birthday each year, and had never been out of touch with her through the years, even during the war, by letter, by messenger, with a hundred little kindnesses, but had now been married for forty years to a woman who had ridden by on her bicycle and found him bleeding in the street, a former piano student.

Being a romantic at heart, Mrs. Leary encouraged Lucia not to give up on the one who she knew would always love her.

"True love will find a way," she assured Lucia, not knowing what else to say. She knew this very well, as Mr. Jim Leary with his taste for clasping her against himself, like gum on the shoe, had done just fine for her for every one of these many years.

Gazing as she had always done down the gravel tree-lined lane which led, for Lucia, never out, only in, Lucia would often remind Nurse Leary, "Look for Charlie Chaplin. Look for Napoleon."

Skewered with curiosity, Mrs. Leary asked timidly, "Who was he? What happened? Who were all those other men?" Then she would squirm because it struck her as sinful to know more than one lover. "Write an essay about him, dearie, get it off your chest," she suggested, hoping to satisfy her own nosiness.

"No!" Miss Joyce refused. "But I will write an essay about you. About how you sleep on the left, Mr. Leary always on the right. How your hand is always between . . ."

"Stop!" Mrs. Leary snapped. But she thought, "Yes, she's right, but how on earth does she know these things?"

Lucia was finally permitted the use of a pen and Mrs. Leary purchased a new fountain pen, filled it, and presented it to her. Lucia unscrewed the top, saw that the point was inky, and cleaned it on her left elbow in the way she had always seen her father do. It left a line and a blot. Sometimes while lining up with the other patients to take her medication, the floor smelling of acidic Jayes Fluid, she would unscrew the pen top and clean the point on her elbow. She and the other patients would joke about it, calling her a blotting-paper lass, but if a nurse or a doctor came near the joking would stop. Quite often, to pass the time and add some astonishment to the unremarkable hospital day, Lucia would tell the others on the line long-forgotten stories from their individual childhoods.

A new parade of scholars and biographers came calling on Lucia. They made her feel important. They bombarded her with questions about her father, about his work. Was she "Issy"? What about the "linkingclass girl"? With reptile eyes they asked very personal questions, which made her head ache even to think about. They asked about money.

After mulling it over for several months, perhaps a year, Lucia announced to Mrs. Leary, "My father was a real writer, you know. I have seen him go about his work and I know how it is done. He wrote two great books.

Bring me a green suitcase to use as a desk! I have written an opera and an essay. Now I will write a memoir. It will be true and not true and keep them guessing for three hundred years. Remember my father and I swam to the bottom of the same river. Though I made the catastrophic mistake of stopping dancing, I am and have always been a true artist at heart."

She locked Mrs. Leary with her mismatched eyes. "Will you read what I write, Sister? Read on your squeaking rocking chair?" she asked.

"I will," replied Mrs. Leary sincerely, feeling a wave of shame that Lucia somehow knew about her squeaky, creaky rocking chair. Was there anything she didn't know?

"My mother meant to read my father's work, I'm sure. She did read up to page twenty-seven counting the cover. My mother liked a leg-pull too. A joke was a joke in our house. Will you correct it before Mother sees my mistakes? I learned English quite late, you know."

Lucia began to write with the new pen on a green suitcase afternoons after tea hour during the loneliest hours in an institution of the type of Barnaderg Bay, between tea and bed—the dark and gloomy, often wet hours of the day for half the year, and the poignantly light and melancholy, also often wet hours of the day during the second half of the year.

She wrote daily from late in 1967 until 1974, sometimes a paragraph or two, sometimes just three or four words at a time.

Tardive dyskinesia, one side effect of long-term use of

antipsychotic medication, slowly began to creep up on her. By 1971 it had gone beyond involuntary muscular movements in her neck and face, her tongue constantly moving around her mouth. Finally it reached her hands and fingers. Soft jerking and purposeless movements began and she could no longer put pen to paper. She stopped writing.

Not to upset her, Mrs. Leary, who had, as promised, read each and every word that Lucia had written and had corrected what she could, especially the word "idol" which Lucia always spelled "idle," gathered the writing up, wrapped the stack with a wide elastic band, and put it with her umbrella. Though the incandescent phrase "for the sake of history" still reverberated, more than anything else the writing was to her a poignant keepsake of her many, many years' friendship with dear old Miss Joyce, who had truly evolved into the cherished sister she had never had.

Time was running out now, their days of camaraderie were numbered. They were both getting quite old.

Nurse Leary gave Miss Joyce a whole box of Black Magic chocolates, Flakes, and two rolls of Roundtree pastilles to take her mind off the memoir, which would now not be completed. She tried to haul her down to the exercise room, but Lucia only complained, "What for? I don't want to jump up and down and swing my arms with all those big fat ladies."

Lucia never asked for the writing, and Mrs. Leary didn't bother about it either because now her thoughts were almost constantly on her own retirement. There would be a party at the local hotel. Everyone would sign a book with either a poem, limerick, or ditty. She would be presented with a gift: a Waterford crystal vase, she hoped. Lucia and several other high-functioning patients would be invited. Her discussion with Lucia Joyce turned from boyfriends to what to wear, and would the lawyers spring for a new dress and a new pair of shoes?

V

At Twenty

The Story of the Blotting-Paper Girl
(Keep Them Guessing for
Three Hundred Years)

A Memoir by Lucia Joyce

I

B Y *DANCING* I broke the string that tied my big toes together. Six hours a day or more, every day for three years. Cours Jaques Dalcroze, Cours Jean Borlin, Cours Madika, Cours Raymond Duncan, Cours Egorova, Cours Lois Hutton and Hélène Vanel in rhythm and color, Cours Margaret Morris in modern dance. Endless classical dance. Performances, recitals as well. I was inhaling dance like oxygen and truly was a dancer.

Wrung out like laundry, each day I returned home to our Square Robiac flat, which had old Dublin all over the walls and even the corkscrew River Liffy woven into a rug on the floor.

It was my own idea to be a dancer, an artist, not my father's and certainly not my mother's. I didn't want it known in my classes who my father was. I was never absentminded about dance.

In November 1926 I danced at the Comédie des Champs-Élysées in a Ballet Faunesque. In February 1927 as La Vigne Sauvage. I was tall. I was limber as hell. Then my adulescentia ended.

2

Even though an American writer had offered to pay tribute to Father by jumping out of a high window, most everyone else was turning against the new book in progress. Only Mother knew its name. By now I had stopped asking him or Mother what the name was. Sean O'Faolain and H. G. Wells didn't like the book in progress. Mr. Pound called it "circumambient peripherisation," Uncle Stanni said it was "driveling rigmarole" and still worse, Miss Weaver called it "unintelligible, a waste of genius."

Father went to bed and didn't get up when Miss Weaver wrote that to him in a letter. Mother shrugged, "Tant pis!" and came home with a marcel wave.

Injections of arsenic and phosphorus were given in Father's eyes because of new eye troubles. I dreamt often of injections, horrific, in the eye. Arsenic, poison, phosphorus, glowing.

In April 1928 at the Théâtre du Vieux-Colombier, I danced the Prêtresse Primitive. When I looked down from the stage, I saw that the audience was filled with white-habited nursing nuns, not a good omen.

Father had a gathering. His friends made me very nervous, but Father wanted me to stay and I did.

Father walked behind me and pointed to a short, stocky man. "Look, he is an onion seller," he told me, points of red standing out on his cheeks. I knew he was superstitious about onion sellers. He thought they brought luck. I think he wanted me to marry an onion seller and have good luck always. This man had a young face, looking like a boy, an angel, but also somewhat half-witted, underdeveloped. He was doing something to his foot, had taken off his shoe. Capillaries decorated his instep with an intricate map of purple and blue figure eights and nines and all the rivers of Canada.

When Father was called to the telephone I counted the Greek flags in a vase on top of the mantel. Then father announced to everyone at the gathering that one among them had to leave at once. The reason was that he had just agreed by telephone to allow an uninvited person to accompany an invited guest, Tom McGreevy, to the gathering. The new addition would bring the number assembled to thirteen, a number he was quite superstitious about, normally for the good, but perhaps not so good at a gathering.

Some of the guests found his urgency laughable but not the onion seller, who took his smelly coat and left. So much for my future husband.

The thirteenth guest was a tall beanpole with glasses named Mr. Beckett. He became Father's helper and began to visit our flat daily. That means every day, rain or shine.

The great author of obscene books, my father, didn't embarrass Mr. Beckett at all. He did the bourgeoisie and I was not invited to their parties by their sons. Tant pis, they would never see my impersonation of Charlie Chaplin.

3

As Mother's friend Mary Colum said about me, "She's pretty but diffident!" It was not true when I danced.

The year 1929 made me very, very tired. Father was sick, then Mother, invincible mother, was sick. Sick with a word we did not say out loud or even not out loud. A hysterectomy made her weep and weep without stopping. My brother had his debut in April. Two Handel songs but Mother wept before and after. She wept before I went to dance class and at night. How was I to stand it? How was I to dance, which means kick, leap, turnturnturn? How was I to shop when I wasn't allowed to shop alone?

Father wrote his work on large cards, oblivious of the weeping. My brother now belonged to a beautiful woman named Helen Kastor Fleischman, who bought hats from

Agnès. He had forgotten about me, his only sister, and slept away, so didn't hear the weeping any longer.

4

On 28 May 1929 the onion seller finished his work at the produce market at Les Halles, and went walking along the Galerie de Montpensier to look at the small shops, which sold old medals and stamps from around the world. He saw a woman with a small beard and a mustache. He saw that she had mismatched eyes. He wanted to make love to her.

At the arched entrance to the Bal-Bullíer he showed a ticket to the usher. She was a little old woman with a black lace collar and a deathly white face and wrists.

A vision appeared on the stage. A live mermaid. She swayed and undulated to the music, a tall, silver-and-green iridescent mermaid with ribbons threaded through her reddish hair. She wriggled across the stage. As the mermaid shimmered in the stage light an underwater effect was created.

The mermaid's dance finished, her tender and lovely face glowed pink as the sound of the hands hitting each other and voices cheering burst from the audience. She was not at all diffident. This man was afflicted with a feeling light and pleasurable, weightless as a rib. His heart had melted totally.

As she bowed gracefully he saw that the silvery scaled

fishtail curled to the left and that a human leg and foot stood beside it.

"Nous réclamons l'irlandaise!" two voices shouted from the crowd. One voice was Father's, the other Mr. Beckett's.

Other voices unknown to me shouted it again, "Nous réclamons l'irlandaise!"

My intuition told me that a stamp had come into the onion seller's mind, one he had seen in a shop on Galerie de Montpensier.

"L'irlandaise! L'irlandaise!" I heard from the audience.

The onion seller saw the mermaid's face go pink with pleasure, her smile contagious to both of her bright blue antelope eyes and to her sweet mouth, with which she was trying to maintain reserve.

Then the lights went out.

Another dancer and another music began.

This was some kind of competition between all the dancers. The onion seller would give his life for his mermaid to win.

I was that mermaid but I did not win.

5

The onion seller followed me out of the theatre. Anxious excitement, perhaps danger, quickened my heavy heart. He backed up and down the curb thirteen times.

Down the street a café had turned on its gramophone. "Pars, sans te retourner, pars."

Then he glimpsed a long, slender green coat, and a long, milky neck. I was walking with a forlorn droop, wearing a helmet-shaped hat pulled way down over my face. I walked with three other people, a blind man, a beanpole, a worshiped mother, but apart.

I was near the corner. The gas lamp turned my coat to green blotting paper.

6

What was the use? My glaring deformities, the strabismus eye, scar on my chin, I could go no further. A dancer must be strong. I was not strong any longer, my deformities took enormous strength from me. There were men everywhere, stimulating, vibrant men. A dancer is like a fighter—sex and training do not mix.

No matter who I went with, Mr. Beckett saw me at home every single day.

I had no choice. I gave up dancing.

Then I began to weep and weep. I wept much more than Mother had wept.

7

I wanted to take Liam O'Flaherty with me to see *Guillaume Tell* at L'Opéra but Mr. Beckett went instead, Mother, Father, Giorgio, and Helen, all of us. I noticed a woman dressed in black silk and wearing a monocle.

I noticed the onion seller dressed in opera clothes, a midnight-blue silk-lined opera cloak and silk hat, which sat on the top of his head as his head was oversized. The suit hung on his short frame, he looked like my beloved Charlie Chaplin.

My lips trembled as I heard the soft rolling kettledrum. I could watch the onion seller two rows ahead, though my knee rested against Mr. Beckett's bony long leg. Swooning into the music I stopped breathing. Then came the piccolo, the French horn, the fanfare of trumpets. And "Galop."

8

The next day the newspaper said, "On 30 June 1930 during a performance of *Guillaume Tell* at L'Opéra . . . the audience was witness to a dramatic scene which exceeded in intensity the drama being played on stage. A sudden hush fell . . . when a man in one of the boxes whom many recognized as James Joyce, the Irish novelist and poet, dramatically leaned forward, raised a pair of heavy dark glasses from his eyes, and exclaimed: "Merci, mon Dieu, pour le miracle. Après vingt ans, je revois la lumière."[1]

Voila! The power of music.

9

Fouquet's appeared imposing to the onion seller. His eyes had searched for me during the love duet of Mathilde and Arnold in the forest. When Guillaume Tell shot and killed a man who fell headfirst into the lake I heard the onion seller scream.

Now he pressed his nose against the cool window glass at Fouquet's. Right off he could see Father at a centrally placed table set for six in a row. Father wore tinted dark glasses. His hair was carefully combed. He was wearing a fine tailored suit and necktie. Mother had reddish brown carefully coiffed hair; had thick eyebrows. She was larger than was Father. Next to her was an empty seat and beside that Mr. Beckett and a younger version of Father, then beautiful Helen. Mother was cutting up the food on Father's plate as Father smoked a cigarette. On Father's hand were three rings; one with an opaque green stone almost exactly like the stone the onion seller held in his fist in his own pocket for luck except blue not green.

A man and woman had come up behind him and were looking over his head through the window. They jabbered on in French. His silk opera cape was slipping off. Then he heard the man say, "C'est un salaud, une ordure, un pornographe, James Joyce," and they laughed and he recognized the word "garbage" and "pornographer." They moved on and he again pressed his nose to the glass. The empty chair was now occupied. There, now in a row, sat the sixth member of Mr. Joyce's group. She sat with a very straight back. She was staring off into space, her eyes slightly mismatched.

She had her mother's eyes but otherwise looked like her father beside her.

He had found his mermaid again. *C'est moi!*

I snapped out of my blank reverie and could see his face looking in at me through the glass.

1 0

The onion seller learned that his mermaid was named Lucia Joyce. That I was twenty-three years old and had in 1923 while at a summer camp outside of Paris met King Alfonso of Spain.

The onion seller often wandered north to the statue of Le Roi Soleil astride his horse, flanked by Prudence and Justice, at the Invalides. He would touch the horse for luck and continue on to touch, for more luck, the winged horses of the Pont Alexandre III, the site of my boyfriend Émile's opera, then would spit seven times into the Seine.

He could often cadge bits of gossip true or false about my family. People in Paris liked to talk about us. Among other things he heard that my father swam in the Seine winter and summer, once a day; that he wore a white doctor's coat while he wrote, and black gloves to bed at night; that he wore four watches at once; that he once had owned cinemas in Trieste; that his writing during World War I while in exile in Zürich was all in codes; that when he was a boy, after his mother's funeral, he had got up in the middle of the night and seen the ghost of his dead mother; that both he and his wife hated umbrellas; that I had a multitude of boyfriends pursuing me, most of whom my parents did not approve. He learned that my parents had run away from Ireland together many years before; that because of years in Trieste my father had chosen Italian, the language of love, as the language of our home.

I had no name for him, only a face. Again I was looking at this man and pressing my leg against Mr. Beckett under the table.

I I

Shortly afterward we met again and I learned his name. This is how.

Soft rain had been falling that night and from a window the onion seller had been watching the slanted silver across the yellow glow of the gas lamp. He watched as a gaggle of young people began to pour down the street toward the front door. He heard the sound of the door opening, then the echo of voices in the foyer.

He continued to watch the rain as a gust of wind turned the slattern raindrops into silver drops of confetti swirling against the light.

He saw that a couple walked haltingly behind the others, that I, wearing a dark fashionable coat, was bareheaded and stopped on the sidewalk to engage in conversation with Mr. Beckett.

My fingers kept pointing up toward the sky at something. He could not see what. Mr. Beckett looked down at the ground, pinched a glowing cigarette between his fingers and dropped it into a puddle at his feet, grinding at the butt long after it must have been shredded.

The tilt of my head and straight back had been his clue. It was me. His mermaid. If only he could fly down from the window and lift me gently into his arms, cover me with his own body, fly me to a safe, dry place and roaring fire and towel me dry with big Turkish towels.

I first noticed him again with pleasure as he entered the room wearing the same opera cloak lined in midnight-blue silk. His dark hair glistened as though it was wet, the brush marks wedge-shaped, cutting the thick hair in rows, his large, dark eyes like glowing coals as he searched the room for me.

Our host came and pounded him on the back and I noticed that he was breathing as though he'd been running.

Mr. Beckett and I had entered the room and sat down. The onion seller observed me, tall and slender, so distracted that I sat on the sofa, shaped like a comma, squinting off into space at something far away that he could not see. He saw that my rapid-fire, flighty talk tumbled out on and off between moments of distraction.

He heard me speak in Italian and halting French. I never seemed to look in a direction toward which I was addressing. He saw the scar on my chin. He thought it made me more beautiful.

He studied my face, my creamy skin, the long fingers of my hands. Though slim, I had full breasts. I seemed to vacillate between comfort and discomfort like a bird hopping from branch to branch.

I was asked to play something on the piano. Mr. Beckett and I discussed what I should play. Sheet music was brought, thumbed through, discussed again. Finally I made my choice, sat down, and then asked the room at large for someone to turn the pages for me.

Like a newborn lamb this man walked the few feet to the piano. He looked at me. I responded with something resembling a greeting, but to him something better, as though an angel had brushed against his heart. A chair was brought and placed just behind me and to the left. The host introduced him to me as Edgar Anthagros, a Greek Jew working in the produce market in Paris. Ezra Pound, who had now also turned against Father, had once turned the pages for Olga Rudge, and now Mr. Anthagros would do the same for me.

I touched the keys with my fingertips, the piano emitted a fragment of melody. Edgar looked at the score. It read "Prelude of Tristan and Isolde." This meant nothing to him, I could see from his blank face.

Then I put my fingers to the keys in earnest and began to play.

I told the music to speak to Mr. Beckett of love—lifelong and eternal love—but it spoke to Edgar instead. Edgar lowered his face down almost into my hair. My hair smelled of rainwater. He longed to bury his face in my hair. I wish he had; I wouldn't have minded.

12

Mr. Anthagros followed me to a beauty salon on the Right Bank. I was wearing a pretty dress and emerged with a new hairdo and painted face and walked with quite a happy gait. He followed me for a mile, finding it difficult to keep up with me.

I entered the Luxembourg Gardens past the Medici fountain, tossing a coin into the shaded pool as I passed. Crossing the street I waved happily at Mr. Beckett standing in front of an Italian bistro. Then I noticed a forgettable second man whom Mr. Beckett had introduced me to. Seeing the second man, my shoulders slumped. Anthagros heard something like the name "Carr" from the distance and heard me say, "Mr. Beckett. Why?"

My composure shriveled, my hands began to tremble. By the time Edgar had come to the restaurant, I was seated in a banquette with the two men. My blank stare off into an abyss. Mr. Anthagros took off his hat and entered the restaurant. He was given a menu and, not taking his eyes off me, pointed at "Saumon Fumé avec Vodka."

Quickly a plate and a glass were brought and placed on his table. Slices of pink fish were arranged in a fan shape on a plate with a scattering of onion rings and a sprig of something green. Anthagros pointed at the indeterminable green before the waiter had gone and the waiter informed him, "Seaweed."

Anthagros gulped down the chilled liquid in the delicate stemmed glass. It burned like kerosene.

I was dissolving into disarray. I looked as though I had slept in my clothes. My lipstick had daubed off to the side of my mouth. The men ate their food while I pushed mine around on my plate.

Suddenly, in my condition of deep abstraction, I rose up like a sleeper and without a word left the restaurant. Mr. Anthagros threw down some money.

He scrambled up, took a handful of salt, and walked behind the banquette where the two men remained looking aghast. He flung the salt at the men. The tall beanpole, Mr. Beckett, stood up with a most helpless look on his face. In Greek Anthagros shouted, "May you have boils." Anthagros spat at his feet. "You green-eyed devil!" He then turned and left the restaurant.

Anthagros glimpsed me entering the Luxembourg Gardens. Still in my trance I retraced my steps from earlier. He quickly caught up to me and, although I was oblivious of him, he walked beside me, his hand lightly, imperceptibly on my elbow.

I made my way back to the Medici fountain pool beneath the stone Renaissance altar and the great stone raging Polyphemus forever poised in his jealous pose, cannonball-sized rock about to crush and obliterate his beloved Galatea and her beautiful Sicilian lover, the shepherd Acis.

I climbed into the shaded pool and knelt down, soaking

my entire dress. I searched for something on the bottom of the pool.

A double line of minute French schoolgirls in uniforms led by a stern sister marched by in orderly fashion, not daring to look at the lady in the pool. Edgar held on to a button until they passed.

I stood up, my dress dripping. I held something in my hand. Still in a trance I reached out my hand and deposited dix centimes into Anthagros's outstretched hand.

1 3

The Rivals

Alexander Calder and I had a love affair. I called him Sandy. He wanted to take me far away to America from where he came. He was the creator and ringmaster of a miniature circus. I never saw him around Paris without a roll of wire across his shoulder and a pair of pliers in one of his pockets in order to shape acrobats, trained dogs, trapeze artists, lion tamers in action, and even Josephine Baker, out of wire for his circus. Out he would roll a slab of green carpeting while his audience (his friends) would squeeze on and around his bed, for his circus was performed in his studio which was also his bedroom. When the carpet was out, the ring would be set down, trapeze poles raised, and a Victrola record would announce, "Mesdames et messieurs . . ."

Out of wire and string he had also made a gadget that would open his front door wide while he lay soaking in his bathtub.

Alex Ponisovsky gave Father lessons in Russian. He had a degree in economics from Cambridge University. He proposed to me.

Mr. Beckett was Irish, not a smiler. He was Oblomov except when he was at our flat.

Émile Fernandez, a nonorthodox Jew, was a jazz musician and something of a composer of music. He had been a Dada and surrealist, and wrote poems. He had proposed to me and I knew I could marry him whenever I chose.

Albert Hubbell studied art. Together we saw *Boris Godunov* and later I danced in his arms. He was a writer. We were having an affair. He was a married man but he and his wife were estranged.

Edgar Anthagros imagined me in his bed night and day.

14

Edgar had been away from Greece for so long he couldn't remember his mother. He only remembered her thumbs, small but capable of strong pressure. He remembered that she had no teeth, a voice that broke with strong feeling, that she almost never smiled but when she did she would hold up her hand to cover her mouth.

Lucia meant light.

The crash in 1929 came.

Father was in a taxi collision because he had seen two nuns.

My brother Giorgio lost his voice.

Mr. Beckett arrived every dash at our door.

My family was moving away from our Square Robiac home. We lived in one hotel and then another.

I had Albert Hubbell at night, Mr. Beckett in the day. I had others. Men I wanted to rub. It rained the entire spring of 1930.

1 5

Edgar and I went into the woods together. I explained *Guillaume Tell* to him. He listened silently, not comprehending any of it. Lucky he hadn't seen *Boris Godunov*. As he listened a little brown rabbit scurried out of the woods and over to him, crouching at his feet. In rapid succession several more rabbits joined the first. Absentmindedly, Anthagros petted the head of one of the rabbits and then took another into his hands.

I slid my singers down the front of his trousers. "Will you be my official page turner?" I asked him.

1 6

"Yes," he replied.

He told me how he imagined himself as a page turner of

the greatest skill. He imagined that as I played the piano,
my long fingers pouring like thick cream across the piano
keys, my ginger hair, like a lion's mane, also poured and
swirling above my head, brushing his wrist electrically as
he turned each page, touching his lips as he rose from his
chair for turnings. His goal as my music tumbled and
rolled, tinkled and reverberated, was to be silent. Silence
and page turning, he said again and again. Silence and page
turning. Lucia, shimmering and music. *Lucia*, an opera.
He fancied himself as the most silent page turner in the
entire history of the world.

I gave him my long green blotting-paper coat. At night
in his dream he could throw it on and go out into the
drizzling night and walk to La Rotonde believing by pre-
monition that my family would be dining in a row. But in
the dream the place was dark. Further down the Boulevard du Montparnasse was La Coupole. A few stragglers
still sat at the bar and one lone woman sat at a table in
the dining room eating quickly from the tail end of a
whole poached fish. Despite the five-meter-high ceiling,
the woman seemed larger than the chair and table and
the waiter, as did the fish. A waiter began to brush off the
banquette beside the lady with a small mustache-like
brush.

In 1927, I told him, near Christmas, despite howling
winds, so many people had come to the opening of this
place that eight hundred cakes, ten thousand canapés and
one thousand pairs of *saucisses chaudes* had been devoured
before dawn, and that the celebrants had drunk up the
champagne so quickly, over fifteen hundred bottles, that

the owner himself had gone out twenty times and returned with a taxi full of more champagne.

I had gone with my brother, when my brother still elonged to me.

He told me another dream he had had. It was 1925. He was dressed in black. He stood on the stage of the Théâtre des Champs-Élysées. He was fourteen years old, his long black trousers, bunched around his ankles, covered his glass shoes, through which his feet could be seen. The theatre was full. He saw my family up in a box staring straight ahead, all four of us wearing black glasses like four blind mice. I sat between my mother and father. My dress was like that of a milking girl. On my lap Edgar could see a small bouquet of white blossoms. Attached to the flow-ers on white silk ribbons flew a handful of white butter-flies, tickling my neck and causing me to wiggle and giggle.

Backstage, Edgar saw that Alan Tanner, a friend of the composer George Antheil, was darning a moth hole in Antheil's tails. Were the butterflies on my bouquet really moths? Had they eaten the hole in the composer's tails?

The title of the piece was *Ballet Mécanique*. The per-formance began. Edgar sat poised to turn the first page. Eight grand pianos were all connected to one piano. That piano began to play cacophonous contortions; hammers, saws, electric bells, xylophones, played along. Edgar saw that no hands were touching the keys, the keys were de-pressing by themselves. There was no score on the piano either. It was a mechanical piano.

Anthagros could hear catcalls behind his back.

Vladimir Golschmann, the conductor, was oblivious of

the catcalls. Edgar dared to look over his shoulder at the
audience and saw that members of the audience were
punching each other. Chaos, except for my family, four in
a row, except for Mr. Eliot and Princess Bassiano,
Adrienne Monnier and Sylvia Beach, and a lady in black
who looked like royalty but turned out to be Sylvia
Beach's concierge.

Then two great plane propellers were turned on and a
shock of cold hit Anthagros's face. His hair stood straight
up. Nevertheless the music continued. He turned again to
the audience. Bedlam had broken out, his eyes searched
out the Joyce box. Father, Mother, and Giorgio had been
blown out of their box, and flew upward. They were
blowing and swirling like autumn leaves, backward, tum-
bling, falling. Only I, holding on to my bouquet with two
hands, was being lifted, exalted, by the team of hard-
working butterflies. Four pairs of black glasses had been
dislodged and tumbled down toward the stage, falling into
the mechanical piano. My butterflies flew me up into the
heavens. Edgar's hand reached out toward the piano and
turned a page with a black border like a death announcement. On the page was written, "On the day of judgment,
blood will come from between the piano keys."

After he told me, I nodded. He was right. I had been at
this concert with my family but I couldn't remember
blood coming out from between the piano keys.

1 7

Émile Fernandez had written the music for *Le Pont d'Or*, an *opérette-bouffe* also at the Comédie des Champs-Élysées, in which I had danced in 1928. It was about an American who fell madly in love with the Czar Alexandre III Bridge. Together, the bridge and the American had a baby that was a boat. That was the story, something like that.

Émile was mad for Negro music and knew many Negroes around Paris, even Josephine Baker. He was very good luck too, a Greek Jew from Salonika like Edgar, but he and his family were rich and, like us, spoke Italian at home. He was afraid of thunder just as Father and I were.

I had come to know him through his sister Yva, a dancer like me, also a pianist like me but much more intellectual than Émile and I.

I turned his marriage proposal down but we continued on and off to keep company. I always thought I could marry him if I ever wanted to, but in 1931 Émile Fernandez, a nonpracticing Jew, converted to Catholicism but was not baptized.

Soon after, he married a Catholic woman in Tuscany and began to study law.

Father would have nothing more to do with him after that, after he went off and out of the blue married someone else.

1 8

Albert Hubbell reconciled with his estranged wife. Good-bye.

1 9

Oblomov told me that when he came to our flat every day it was not to see me, it was to see Father.

He told me this to my face.

Father banned him from coming ever again to our flat.

Mother and Father thought that he had behaved like a cad and that my heart was broken. It was, if loss of all four corners is a broken heart.

2 0

Jules Pascin, the Jewish painter, committed suicide in Paris in June. My brother and I slightly knew Jules. Originally from Bulgaria, he had lived in Vienna and then gone to study art in Munich, and in his many night reveries at Café du Dôme my brother had often seen him.

I had been invited to the opening of Pascin's new exhibition at the Galerie Petit. Instead, we all drank with Lucy Krohg, his lover, who had found Pascin hanging in his studio and had laid his body beside his painting "The Raising of Lazarus." With his own blood, from slices cut into his wrists, Pascin had written, "Adieu, Lucy" across the door to his studio. Not wanting it to upset me, my brother didn't tell me all the details about the suicide. I was not allowed by my mother to go to funerals. I became swollen by the image of Pascin's painting "Socrate et Ses Disciples Conspués par les Courtisanes."[2]

In my mind I saw the face of Pascin rather than Socrates being mocked by the plump, naked, entwined courtesans, me among them. Ten years before, Amadeo Modigliani, the most elegant of all the artists in Paris, had died on the ward of a charity hospital at age thirty-six of tubercular meningitis, weakened by love of alcohol and drugs. The tragedy compounded when his lover, Jeanne Hebuterne, committed suicide the following day.

This happened before I knew any of these people but no one ever seemed to forget Modigliani, this tragic Italian Jew. I hoped people wouldn't forget Pascin and Lucy, or any of us who didn't leave France alive.

2 1

Mr. Anthagros took up a vigil outside our hotel, always in his too-long trousers; I likened him to Charlie Chaplin.

When Father emerged from the hotel, he would acknowledge Edgar's vigilance with a tilt of his head and a loosening tension of his hand on the knobby tip of his walking stick as he strode off up the street, either alone, oftimes with his companion, a Russian Jew, Paul Léon, who had long ago converted to Catholicism, or Mother, Giorgio, Helen, me, us all, when they would take me with them at night. Father had nothing but praise for Edgar.

Often at night Edgar would observe Mother returning home alone and still later he'd see Father carried home like a sack of potatoes by one of his friends.

I went to an exhibition of the paintings of Maria Lani, a famous German actress who had been brought to Paris by two impresarios, the Abramovicz brothers who had persuaded all the best artists in Paris—over fifty of them—to paint the star's portrait gratis. I had never seen her famous films or theatre work and assumed that I was too sheltered with dancing and with Mother and Father's life. My brother attended the exhibition, taking me with him.

At the exhibition I was drawn to a portrait by young Marc Chagall, a Russian in exile, who was also illustrating the Bible. Chagall had adorned Maria Lani with a grand Nefertiti coiffure. Woven into the hair, the Eiffel Tower. A good idea, *n'est pas?*

The exhibition was a smash.

Shortly afterward, Maria Lani and the Abramovicz brothers and the dozens of portraits quietly and mysteriously vanished from Paris.

Then word traveled across Paris that the "star" Maria Lani from Germany was really a Prague stenographer, and that the "film impresarios" the worldly Abramoviczes were merely her husband and her brother.

The final word was that the stenographer and her husband and brother and all the paintings, sculpture, and musical tributes had sailed for America.

All of Paris had been had. The world depression was reaching Paris also. Antiforeign decrees were putting pressure on all non-French. We were all becoming fools over what to do about it.

22

When my engagement to Alex Ponisovsky was announced in March 1932 I couldn't feel love for Alex. But I did want to be married because my mother had been pinned against a gas lamp by an out-of-control bus.

Father had been furled. His own father had died leaving him fatherless and at the mercy of all omens. "She's clairvoyant," he told Mother about me.

He explained that I knew something extremely important and was trying to awaken them all. He looked for messages in my flights of thought in conversation, in my distractions.

Regardless, my brother took me to a *maison de santé*.

23

Our family moved to London. Forever. Where was London?

24

Like a jewel I showed new and incompatible sides, which were breaking off from each other, but diamonds are diamonds.

I watched a girl dressed in my clothes throw a chair at Mother's italics on the day of Father's fiftieth birthday on 2 February 1932.

I saw a girl dressed like me become engaged to Alex Ponisovsky at a big party at Drouand's restaurant then go to the home of Lucie and Paul Léon on the rue Casimir Périer and stretch herself out on the sofa. I lay this way, taking doses of Veronal and phosphate of lime in a catatonic pose, isolated and paralyzed with the weight of so much clairvoyance, while Father blamed Paul Léon for encouraging this engagement.

A girl dressed like me was seized by a vision at the Gare du Nord.

Another girl dressed like me while staying with Mother's closest friend Mary Colum slept with her nightdress pinned to that of Mrs. Colum.

Giorgio tricked me and got me to get into a taxi, which took me to a *maison de santé*. This time in L'Hay-les-Roses where the doctor, Dr. G. Maillard, labeled my feverish clairvoyance "hebephrenia."

Knowing better, Father was convinced that soon all others would come to realize the voices being spoken by girls dressed like me were other people's voices trying to be heard, not my own. He blamed everyone for instigating

my state and all men especially who had betrayed me.
Mother particularly blamed Mr. Beckett.

2 5

My name for Father was L'Esclammadore. Although he
sighed and was silent much of the time, he would also
exclaim, "Già!," which he had used with us since I was a
small child in Trieste when only Italian was spoken by our
family at home.

Edgar saw Father at Fouquet's through the window and
knew we had returned from London but I was not with
him. Father had smuggled me away from the *maison de
santé* and I had gone with a nurse for a rest to Feldkirch
in the Austrian Alps, to a chalet. Father and Mother had
stayed nearby in Zürich but had now returned to Paris. I
would be working on some letter designs there, which
Father called *lettrines*. Father showed Anthagros a beautifully decorated letter, which he asked to keep for luck.
Father agreed. Anthagros placed the sheet of paper next to
his skin beneath his undershirt.

Shortly afterward Mother went and stayed with me at
the chalet in the Alps where I had gone. Father joined us
despite new troubles with his failing eyes. Father was
thinking of abandoning his book or of leaving it filled with
blanks.

My parents and the nurse and I had another holiday in
France. Then the nurse and I went to Vence, and Mother

and Father went on to Nice until we all returned to Paris. Father assured Edgar that I, now no longer engaged, was turning again into an inspired artist.

Father bought me a new fur coat. Although I no longer danced, I was writing, painting, and bookbinding. My talents, unlike those of Father, who could only write and sing, were unlimited. I had studied piano for three years in Zürich and Trieste, singing in Paris and Salzburg, and drawing at the Académie Julian here in Paris also.

Unfortunately my doctors were not convinced by my productivity and I was made to drink seawater. In sympathy Mr. Anthagros also drank seawater for a month, and Father suffered from various imaginary afflictions.

Edgar and Father walked in the rain one afternoon after the New Year of 1933 had arrived. Father stood quietly while Edgar drew the letter *o* with his foot. He made no reply when Edgar asked him, "When can Lucia hold a baby in her arms?"

Instead of replying Father held out both hands and watched the quicksilver raindrops gather between his long, tapered, nicotine-stained fingers. Then he sang in a sorrowful tenor's voice, "Era una piccola bambina che rideva durante il giorno e non dormiva durante la notte."[3]

2 6

A series of new friends were being provided for me by Mother and Father and Giorgio.

While they thought I was resting in bed Anthagros and I would roam the city together. Music streamed between us. *Tristan and Isolde.* We were happy while the music streamed.

I took E. A. by train to Munich. It was late at night when we arrived. I made the taxi driver take us to look at the grand Prinzregenten Theatre. I explained the romantic link between Wagner and the Bavarian capital to Edgar. I told him that the world premiere of *Tristan and Isolde* had taken place at the baroque Residenz Theatre. I told the taxi driver to take us there. I didn't tell him that I was not certain of this. Then the driver deposited us at the Hotel Vier Johreszeiten. We were too agitated to sleep and left the hotel and roamed together through the city throughout the night.

Although it was just the end of September, there was such frost that a white ring totally encircled the moon. We wandered into a chilling maze of shabby cafés and Edgar sat down on the curb. He took off his shoe, felt inside for a stone, found none, removed his sock and shook it out.

We heard voices haranguing from the backroom of one of the cafés. Nothing fell out of his sock.

Suddenly E. A. burned with fever and the Canadian rivers on his instep froze blue. By the time we reached the Königsplatz he shook with fever and was twisted into a knot.

At dawn E. A. had turned a bloodless blue from the chills. He rubbed himself with turpentine and made himself drink a cup of kerosene which he remembered as the cure for yellow fever.

2 7

We took a train to Vienna. From our taxi we drove past long breadlines. I purchased armloads of flowers and we went to the cemetery and laid flowers on Beethoven's grave. Then Schubert's and Haydn's and Brahms's. Finally on the grave of Johann Strauss and Hugo Wolf. I placed the last armload of lilies on a grave that had been symbolically marked as that of Mozart's though it was not his.

"The Viennese are wicked and they buried Mozart in a common grave out of spite," I told E. A.

He did not know who Mozart was. He grew pious, assuming that I had dead relatives in Vienna. He did not know who else one would pay homage to in a graveyard.

Again his fever rose. Because I had tickets, I left him at the Sacher Hotel submerged in a bathtub filled with chunks of ice and went to the 9 November evening concert at the Musikverein. My last sight of him was blue-skinned and tremorous, wincing because the sharp chunks of ice hurt him.

The concert at the Musikverein was delayed because the pianist found a Viennese-made Bösendorfer piano rather than the old Beckstein that he had been promised.

While I was gone E. A. had a vision of me in a room somewhere, terrified as great claps of thunder sounded. He knew about my terrible fear of thunder.

2 8

E. A. was so weak that when we arrived in Berlin I had to hold him by the hand when crossing the street. He seemed as though he was in a fog, oblivious of automobiles or streetcars. His hand was so hot it burned to hold.

I left him in our room at the Kaiserhof and searched for a hotel doctor. I found a stone-deaf old man with hairy ears, who laboriously made his way to the room and diagnosed the source of the fever as catarrh. "High fever can cause feeble-mindedness," he advised, looking closely at Edgar's face.

The doctor left a foul-smelling, egg-yolk-yellow elixir in a glass beaker.

After he had gone E. A. spat between his fingers to protect him from a spell that the doctor might have placed on him. He had never in his whole life been visited by a doctor. Then he stared unblinkingly at the cabbage-rose wallpaper, watching the sunlight dissolve quickly into a pall of dusk.

He refused to drink the medicine by clamping his chattering teeth shut and rolling his eyes into the back of his head. No one more than I could understand his reluctance. As the evening wore on his body became scalding and rigid to the touch. He whispered to me: "neft," "kepocuh."

I went down to the service desk of the hotel and insisted on turpentine and kerosene.

Obeying his instructions I rubbed his body from neck

to ankle with turpentine, then held a glass half full of kerosene to his parched lips. In three gulps he drank it down.

Not knowing what else to do, I crossed him over his head, stomach, and both shoulders by way of a Russian blessing. We turned on the radio and together listened to Bruckner's Seventh Symphony. Then the Fourth Symphony of Mahler. And several Chopin mazurkas.

E. A. staggered out of bed and pulled at the brocade drapes until they were pulled apart and the gauze curtains beneath had also been pushed and tugged askid. The window faced the Wilhelmstrasse. Again there was a white ring of frost around the moon. I pried open the window for him and a blast of icy night air slapped him across the face. Neither of us saw the dignified façades of embassies and ministries, with snowy roofs and frosted windows, but instead a street of rubble.

I kissed his hand and said, "April."

The fever lifted, and he could feel the cold and gauzy curtains blowing against his cheek like a frozen skin, which he could easily have snapped in two.

He blinked and his eyes and lashes were iced. We saw that a new ice rain was falling.

"In fifteen Aprils you will be safe in France," he assured me, and then asked, "Before fifty Aprils have passed will you become my bride?"

"Of course." I replied laughing, relieved to the point of giddiness, and both of us suddenly ravenously hungry for food and sex at the same time.

We made love, stuffed whole loaves of bread into our

mouths, and made love and ate again and again to the point of total satiation.

On the morning train back to Paris I commented that neither E. A. nor I knew Russian, but Russian words and ways had visited us.

2 9

In a couple we made another journey.

We found ourselves in a hilly park in Linz on the Danube, the snow deep. About one in the morning the wind abated and the moon rose. We didn't know how we had got there. I pulled a branch from a linden tree and we slogged up a hill, going deep into the park to a clear, level place.

Carefully Edgar removed the sheet containing my *lettrine* and studied the design in the ivory moonlight. Then, with total precision, he drew a perfect replica of my design in the snow with his stick, only on a scale of one hundred to one.

The moon was totally up by the time he finished. It cast a luminous albedo of light across the gigantic decorated letter *o*. Edgar saw what looked like an ocean of salt. Finally he drew a four-sided border around the design. It looked like a giant, ornate playing card.

Our clothes cracked from the cold. In the distance we heard an Austrian dog growling, its chain rattling in the silent park. Afraid of dogs, too, he spat between his fingers.

We walked back to a hotel. The cold had turned us blue and the wind again began to howl.

The next day we took the train to Paris but ended up in Italy. By the time the new day had dawned we were in Florence. The sky was bright blue, the sun was pouring down on our heads like hot honey.

Finally we found our way back to Paris, where Edgar took his savings wrapped in a handkerchief and went to the market and bought a North American mockingbird as well as a wicker cage.

I remained in bed.

Edgar stood under my window in the light snow with bird and cage in front of our new apartment on rue Galilée. He knew that I was fast asleep above him. He whistled a few notes from the "Prelude" at the bird and, sheltering the cage from the wet flakes of snow floating lightly, he waited for the bird to sing, but the bird was silent.

Again, the following night, the bird was still.

On the third night, before setting out for the rue Galilée, with an eye dropper Anthagros patiently fed the bird drops of pale emerald absinthe. Barely had they reached the rue Galilée when the bird began to sing the "Prelude."

Not only did the bird sing the melody, but it improvised and expanded the themes, and with full throat sang at the top of its voice.

All night the bird sang. Whenever it slowed down, Edgar fed it a few droppers more of absinthe, and the bird, refreshed, would sing again.

Edgar imagined that above him I slept. He hoped that the bird's sweet voice would enter the window and surround my sleeping body; that the song would ward off my recent visions of gobbets of children's flesh being served up by Atreus as he quietly turned each page.

Through January and February Edgar kept the bird singing beautifully at night for his mermaid. Unfortunately, quickly the bird became completely addicted and had to be fed absinthe every two hours or it agitated and shook.

Outside a shop one afternoon when Edgar had gone to buy more absinthe, a man with creases of worry between his eyes, carrying a small suitcase, pulled Anthagros's coat sleeve with large, coarse hands. The man looked first to the left and then to the right and then leaned down and whispered into Anthagros's ear in English that he had a dead white rabbit in his suitcase that he had accidentally strangled and that he didn't know what to do with it, how to dispose of it.

As Edgar did not know English, he thought, because of the suitcase, that he was being asked directions to the railway station. Taking the man by the arm, he walked him carefully to the Gare de l'Est. When the stranger put out his hand to shake in thanks, Edgar saw that his hands weren't large nor were they coarse. They were small and smooth, only clumsy like the entire man. The man's eyes were deep ultramarine.

He was unable again to find the emerald elixir La Fée Verte,[4] which had been banned since 1915, that made the bird sing its best. Distraught, Edgar went to his room and reread all his mother's letters to him, going backward in time. He kept the letters tied together by a gray piece of twine and wrapped in cloth in an old chocolate tin with the face of a cat on the top. He remembered how in Genti Couli his mother dried her herbs above the chimney. He recalled the red neck of his grandfather, on which the sun had beaten down for seventy years.

3 0

Edgar Anthagros captured a bluebottle and trapped it in the chocolate box with the letters. He made breathing holes with an awl and hammer and listened to the metallic buzzing against the tin. Because the bird would not sing as richly after drinking ordinary Pernod, Anthagros ceased to bring him to my window to sing at night. Instead he would arrive at the first light, when sound seemed to him to carry twice as far with added poignancy. Or was it tenderness?

Because I had so often been ordered by my doctors to lie quietly close to an open window—after being given phosphate of lime and doses of smelly Veronal again— Anthagros's idea was for the bird's song to reach and soothe my bruised nerves. It would be better, he decided, if these new friends being provided for me encountered the refreshed, natural Lucia rather than any of the false impostors, diamonds or not. There was an architect among these new friends. Anthagros hoped that such a man wouldn't design my dreamed-of house as he had his own dreamed-of house in the country in his mind for himself and me. It was a country house, but small, with small pens built to house the many rabbits, and a place for the drinking bird.

Edgar festooned a silk evening hat and ebony iron-tipped cane. He had studied father's clothes as he and mother departed from the rue Galilée in evening clothes on the way to the theatre or opera. This is how Anthagros wanted to look.

After I made a horrific scene at the Gare du Nord, I was taken to the asylum Les Rives de Prangins at Nyon, then home again to rue Galilée, where a new companion was installed.

I was much cheered when my parents took me out into the country to visit René and Kathleen Bally, who kept domesticated goats whose hooves had been painted gold. Because I heard sinister warnings being broadcast through the telephone wires in rue Galilée, trying to spoil the many congratulations flooding in for my father because of good news concerning his work, a girl dressed like me cut the telephone wire not once but twice. She attacked my mother with my fists and declared, "C'est moi l'artiste!"

As soon as I could escape, I ran away from the city for three days with Edgar. He took me to the countryside to a peasant's house. Together we walked in the woods, ate and drank, and remained quite calm. Edgar wore his opera cape, I wore my evening gown.

While I played the "Prelude" on a battered accordion I sat on a wooden bench, Edgar sat on the floor beneath me, put his face under my gown, and made love to me with his face. Afterward, gasping for breath, the musicsex ringing in our ears, we listened to voices that spoke to us of a coming storm across all of Europe about to ignite in Austria. The voice spoke to me in Italian and to Edgar in Ladino. We were helpless to alter storms, denied the pleasure of our musical lovemaking by these voices.

The police came and found us. I was accused of wearing evening clothes in the day, and was taken back to Paris to a new flat my parents had found on rue Edmond-Valentin. I then passed whole days at my window, now with bars casting striped shadows across my face. At a distance I could hear droning voices that had come to read aloud to my father, whose eyesight—after sixteen operations—was almost nonexistent.

I was taken again to Prangins to a blood specialist who wished to study me for leucocytosis and to Burghölzli in Zürich for more blood studies and consultation with Dr. Binz Wanger. I demanded that my father smoke a mahogany pipe. Father recognized my clairvoyance not just in my words but in all I did. Though I had collapsed almost into total inertia, Father took me, each day after tea, for a walk through the village square. He would sing to me, softly, almost under his breath so that no one else would hear what he was saying.

> "*C'era una volta,*
> *una bella bambina.*
> *Che si chiamava Lucia.*"

He held me by the arm with one hand, slipping the other around my waist. He wore the royal blue velvet jacket that I loved. I saw that Father's complexion was almost as red as fire.

On a day of anxiety a voice suggested that I light a fire in my room. In obedience I lit not one but four.

I was taken to Küsnacht, also in Zürich, to the great Carl Jung, the Swiss who had commented that father's work could be read backward as well as forward. Father thought the comment more applicable to me, the true innovator in the Joyce family, finding it a compliment rather than an insult. Father was against depth psychology but took me anyway, going against his own principles.

Father counted. In these last difficult years I had needed:

8 companions
11 nurses
24 doctors
a score of *maison de repos*
48 fistfuls of money

I could not tell if all this had happened in ten years or ten days. I got hold of a bottle of black ink and, taking great care, painted my face black. I painted my fingers black as well but left my palms unpainted.

At Küsnacht I learned to play billiards. Each time the black ball collided against another with a sure, clean crack, my head would clear, a curtain of peace would descend, and everything around me would seem very laughable. I could not subdue cascading laughing jags at these times, and tears fell so effusively that the front of my dress would get soaked. Then my mind would light on Parnell. Father had told me that quicklime had been thrown into his eyes, and my mind would grow murky again, the tears would dry on my face. I could not fathom what had caused the front of my dress to be soaking wet.

Both my mother and father liked the opera *La Somnambula*, which they had seen in Trieste together. Or did Mother not like it? Did it make her impatient? Father liked French-style string beans just the way Mother cooked them in Italy, France, or even Switzerland. They always tasted the same.

Because Father was so sentimental, he arranged that the jacket of one of his books duplicate exactly the shade of the Irish Calville apple. On a special day Mother would cook us all her very own favorite dish, rhubarb pudding luxuriously coated with meringue, but sentimental as well she baked apples in the old way for us, enclosed in fluffy pastry. All these memories mixed together in a recipe in my thoughts. I could not understand why my mother was so distraught when she arrived for a late-morning visit and found me dressed in evening clothes. What a dreadful failure I was.

Father and Mother went to hear *Die Meistersinger* and told me the entire story of the opera during a drive they took me on through the mountains around the lake. I in turn told Dr. Jung the story.

I asked him, "My father says that he and I are cut from the same cloth, do you agree?"

"Yes," replied Herr Doktor, "you are both like people sinking to the bottom of the same river."

"Then why am I here in the river not dancing, not singing, not drawing, and why is my father in the river, the calligrapher of books?"

"The difference is that you are falling to the bottom of the river and your father is diving."

"Then help me to dive too, to dance again," I pleaded and Dr. Jung said that he would try.

3 1

Dr. Jung was quite optimistic that there was hope for me. I saw him often and he asked me to tell him many things about Father and me.

I told Herr Doktor that though Father was not a religious man in Trieste he had attended many Greek Orthodox church services, only standing at the back of the church. He did the same in Paris, standing at the rear and listening for the benediction. To him the opera was a sacrament. He would fast before, worship during, and only eat and drink afterward. I told him that I too was not religious but had been designing *lettrines* for Chaucer's "Hymn to the Blessed Virgin" in a medieval style.

I dared not tell the doctor that I had heard my father refer to Dr. Jung as a Swiss Tweedledum, while he called Dr. Freud the Viennese Tweedledee. I dared not tell him that my father had been known to wear four watches all telling different times; or that I was tormented night and day, had been barraged with omens that Europe, perhaps the earth, was soon to be crisscrossed by hobnail boots. This I did not speak about for fear that giving voice to this secret information would release it out into the world, actually cause it to occur. Then I would have been the striker of the cataclysmic match.

Each time it swelled up in my throat and tried to jump out in conversation I would swallow it down and seal my lips with imaginary wire.

Like electric sparks, signals were being sent to me daily. A ticking clock. A drowning bird. A train off the tracks but still gaining speed, hurtling toward a village. Father's book oozing suddenly from my nose. Cackling, conspiratorial laughter under my bed. Men in coats. Women wearing crosses. A window that asked, please, to be broken. A throat that asked to be throttled or bitten like a bunch of grapes. All I could tell Dr. Jung was that I knew I was too small to be a real artist, and that no one would ever love me truly because of the ugly scar on my chin.

"See how many artists are twisted inside out like pretzels; knotted up like roots. I would happily sell shoes or fruit or onions for a two-eyed, simple life," I told Herr Dr. Jung.

I waited for the doctor to assure me. He waited for me to continue speaking.

Thoughts about the end of the world were again gnawing through my skin. The words that Dr. Jung was writing down seemed excessively black, the sound of my voice echoing back and forth in my ears seeming as though it was false and metallic. Was it?

This fat, materialistic Swiss was trying to control my soul.

I refused to speak to him after that.

3 2

"Every day I see new indications of my daughter's clairvoyance," Father earnestly told Dr. Jung.

Dr. Jung shook his head. Father ignored this.

"She is the inventor of a new art form, not I. She has brought innovation to an extraordinary level. No one can understand her, as they couldn't understand me at first, disregarded and derided me, discounted my work, banned my work."

Dr. Jung said that he would not give up but he knew in his heart that he could help me no more.

3 3

I ate Christmas dinner with my parents in Zürich at the Restaurant Kronenhalle. Father sat in an atmosphere of gloom. Mother kept up a steady stream of small talk. I looked from Mother to Father with no comprehension as to which was which and whether or not I was very young or very old.

They drank Fendant de Sion wine. Having known the

family for many years, the owner sent a bottle of Father's favorite Neufchâtel, hoping to dispel the gloom.

I remained lost in silence. I needed to touch the wine glass to make sure it was solid, not soft like cotton wool.

The same went for my own face. Father did not turn the glass of Neufchâtel to see it sparkle in the candlelight.

In the New Year a new nurse moved into the Hôtel Villa Élite as a companion for me. I had been removed from Küsnacht.

Shortly thereafter the nurse and I traveled to London to visit Miss Weaver. Along the way, each time I glimpsed a slim man alone and whistling to himself, with his hat brim turned in a gay way, I walked close to see if it was my father traveling at a discreet distance. The same happened when, on the boat, I saw a long white cane brandished like a rapier by a very young man wearing dirty tennis shoes and oval black glasses, trying to wend his way through the queue at the end of the journey.

My parents had presented me with a new opera cape with white fox fur trim for this trip. I feared that as it had ruined my dancing, my disastrous case of strabismus would totally ruin my life, that the scar on my chin and also the size of my nose precluded any chance of happiness I might have. No beautiful new cloak would help in the slightest. Finding it almost impossible to concentrate or even stir myself from the apathy that had settled over me, I could not even comb my own hair or dress myself.

Miss Weaver was afflicted with a case of shingles. I was being treated by the famous Professor N. Ischlondsky, an expert on regenerative gland treatments who had published a tract in Russia on the gonad glands, for a new diagnosis of glandular imbalances, a deficiency in adrenalin secretion. Two lukewarm, two-hour baths were the treatment. I needed help into both baths and might have spent the entire day underwater if the nurse hadn't returned to pull me out, dry me off, dress me, and help me back to the couch. My hands and feet were wrinkled like old prunes.

The nurse reported to Miss Weaver that I had threatened to buy two pistols. Miss Weaver reported this to Father. I reported to Mother that marriage was the only salvation offered to Hindu girl children because Hinduism said that females arrived on this earth with no souls. But what of me? I was not Hindu and couldn't in good conscience convert!

My hands, I further told Mother, were so distant from my body that I didn't know anymore if they were connected to my body. Were they? Because my own thoughts were being broadcast in my head, I waited until Miss Weaver was out on a business appointment and the nurse was down in the kitchen feeding her always famished appetite, then I grabbed my opera cloak and bolted from the house.

I went as far as I could on a bus. I found myself far from Gloucester Place when I was overtaken by fatigue. I slept where I was, under a street lamp. When the police found me the opera cape was in shreds. Miss Weaver came to the police station to fetch me, and brought me back home. I told Miss Weaver to keep her rules to herself. I demanded to do as I pleased—after all, my father was a famous man.

The doors and windows all now contained locks.

Father was determined to resist any persuasion to put me back into another *maison de santé*. The year was 1935. I was twenty-eight years old. He swore to Mother that their only daughter's mind was lightning quick, and what might be construed as incomprehensible nonsense to others was flashes of imagination and wisdom.

That I threatened suicide put Father into a terribly low state; he too suffered terrible lethargy with his own work. The book he had been working on for fifteen years—his masterpiece, he hoped—seemed no closer to completion. Perhaps, he mused, if he could complete his book, then I too would be freed.

3 4

The strategy was—complete and total freedom. Mother shopped for weeks and prepared two trunks for me. At the same time she bought eleven mirrors for the new flat on rue Valentin. The opera cloak was mended.

My strategy was to effect a reconciliation between my father and the entire country of Ireland. I would travel with my favorite aunt, Aunt Eileen, Father's look-alike sister. Edgar would join me, my father agreed.

Aunt Eileen's strategy was—Irish eggs, Irish air.

Edgar told Lyo, his boss, that he would be going away for a trip. He did not know where, but he would need to eat a salmon that had swallowed a hazelnut before he went.

Mother and Father accompanied me to the boat train for London. There was no scene at the station, the trunks were loaded, I was the Lucia of old—sweet and laughing at every wry comment made by either Father or Mother. My mother thought to herself that I looked too chic to be going to dirty old Ireland, that I should be going to a horse race instead. She didn't say this out loud, having become, she believed, the world champion walker-on-eggs, always alert lest a chair come flying across the room aimed at her head.

Father slipped an Irish pound into Edgar's pocket for luck as Edgar stood off to the side of the tracks, trying as best as he could to adjust his trousers, which seemed to have unequal leg lengths.

After the train had departed, I went to find Edgar. I found him squeezed between two French schoolchildren in a second-class car with all their school books on *his* lap. I brought him back to my compartment. There I presented him with a hatbox. He held the hatbox and slowly turned it with appreciation.

I laughed, "Ouvre la boîte!" He did not understand. I laughed again and pulled off the top. Edgar peered inside. He liked what he saw.

"Charlie Chaplin!" I laughed and removed a black bowler hat from the box. I placed it squarely on Edgar's large head. Though just slightly too small, it made him so happy that he tasted salt in his tears.

In London Aunt Eileen met me and took me by boat to Dun Laoghaire and then twelve more miles further along the coast, to the seaside town of Bray, where she had rented a half bungalow on Meath Road quite close to both the railway station and the sea. I arrived on St. Patrick's Day, I carried a long walking stick like a scepter and wore a grand camel's-hair coat.

Once Aunt Eileen had installed me and gone back into Dublin, I rearranged all the furnishings in anticipation of Edgar's arrival. I put the bottle of Veronal under the mattress, then changed into an oriental kimono with nothing on underneath and lit the gas.

Edgar arrived in the taxi that was bringing the trunks. He saw that the door was wide open and people from the neighborhood were standing at their doors and staring boldly at the half bungalow. I heard someone say, "She squints."

He carried one trunk into the house and the taxi man carried the other. Then he closed the front door. He had stopped along the way and purchased groceries and a bag of large *pamplemousse*, which he now put into a glass bowl and placed in the center of the table.

First he sang a song he'd learned as a child in Genti Couli, the town outside of Saloniki, where he was born.

> *And so ask our bride*
> *What do you call a head?*
> *This is not called a head but*
> *A round grapefruit hanging on a grapefruit tree.*
> *Oh, my grapefruit in a tree,*
> *Oh my spacious countryside,*
> *Long live the Bride and Groom*

We began to eat and he told me about his childhood. He explained that all four of his older brothers had gone to the Transvaal gold mines in South Africa before he was born. His mother had lit candles for their safe return but none had returned. Though he was a small boy during the Great War, Edgar remembered his own father going with a group of men from the village to work in French ship-yards. His father was bearded with blue eyes. He recalled more lighting of candles.

After the Great War Edgar lived with his mother, grandfather, and last three unmarried sisters in a tin house that had been an Allied troop barrack during the war. They waited for their father to return but he did not.

The entire village worked in the shipyards.

Quite young he would feed his mother's silkworms with mulberry leaves and tend to the bright yellow silk loops that emerged from the kettles, wound themselves onto the wooden frames. At night he would fall asleep listening to the crunching, chewing of the silkworms.

When his mother took the raw silk to the loom, Edgar would hold the soft curls carefully for her, reluctant to surrender them to the weavers.

Like a sack of stone he had fallen headfirst from a fig tree and died.

In the family's tin shack a cloth covered the shard of mirror on the wall and an earthen pitcher of clean water stood at the door. Together the men carried the borrowed child's-size pine box to the cemetery. Women sobbed and moaned, prayers were chanted as the procession passed through the narrow streets and up toward the cemetery.

When the noise of a funeral was heard in other parts of town, doors were shut. Behind these closed doors the women in their kitchens, in order to walk symbolically with the dead boy, walked three steps forward and then, in order to return symbolically to normal life (come back from the dead), walked three steps backward.

When they arrived at the cemetery a small grave had been dug. The body was removed from the borrowed casket.

Edgar's grandfather took a handful of dirt, pulled Edgar's eyelids open, and rubbed the dirt into his eyes. Then the men lowered the body into the grave. The grandfather splashed the body with wine, thinking, "This boy will never drink wine. Never love a woman. Never sing a song. Never carry on my name." The rabbi sprinkled the body with dry dirt. Immediately, then, all the mourners began to throw dirt down on the small body below, head and foot. Wailing, the mother covered her own face with dirt.

It was at this moment that Edgar sat up and began to rub his eyes.

Still covered with dirt, he was carried home to his grandfather's bed. His aunt fainted dead out when she saw him carried in through the door. His mother washed him from head to toe and tied a piece of potato with cloth onto his head. She made pinholes in a sheet of newspaper and covered him front and back.

His mother then mixed a glass of water with sugar and went to the fig tree. She poured the mixture into the ground where the accident had occurred. His mother be-

lieved that Edgar had been smitten with the evil eye, perhaps from the dangerous blue eyes of his father.

Daily she chanted seven times:

All the evil eyes, all the stares, the pain and the evil eye
All will go to the bottom of the sea,
And this creature will be freed from the evil eye

Then, morning and night, and between, she would
throw a handful of salt into the stream of his urine, and
say:

They are not from the sky, nor the earth.
How they come, so should they go.

When he got older his roaming ways began. Much of
the city of Thessaloniki, as it was then called, had been
devastated by the great fire in the summer of 1917 and still
lay in ruins. Edgar would climb around the charred re-
mains and up the slopes of Mount Khortiátis, through
huddled houses of the old town, close to the battlement
walks of the old citadel where Mediterranean pine trees
had begun, through the charred woods, to sprout tender
green shoots again.

Sometimes he would go to the Lefkós Pirgos[5] on the
quay of the old port, surrounded by trees that had been
spared by the fire, sit down on the rampart, swinging his
legs above the swells, watching ships sail out to sea.

In winter the eerie Vardar wind would fure and whine
in his ears, but he wandered still.

3 5

When I next opened the door to the bungalow both Edgar and I were fat as Christmas geese. Because this was my first time playing house, I had created my own menus for food—*pamplemousse*, raw meat, and buttermilk scones with cabbage, sweetbreads, and porridge. Neither of us had ever been fat before and we decided that it was to our liking. It made noise seem further away, it made sleeping cozier.

We hired a car and took a trip to Lisdoonvarna Spa and drank from two springs: first from the Rathbaun Spring for iron and manganese, then the Gowlaun Spring for lithium and sulfur. To prolong our health cure we purchased several jars of Ocean Swell carrageen, the mucilaginous dark green seaweed, to bring back to Bray with us.

Back at our bungalow to keep us laughing I recited:

> There was an old woman
> who lived in a lamp;
> she had no room
> to beetle her champ.
> She's up with her beetle
> and broke the lamp
> and then she had room
> to beetle her champ.

while Edgar mashed large bowls of hot cooked potatoes. Together we sprinkled generous shakes of pepper and salt onto the potatoes, added hot milk and hot melted butter and then melted chocolate. We beat and beat until the whole banquet was creamy and fluffy. Then we filled our soup bowls with our invented concoction and sat together, back to back, outside in the little yard, while I read to him sections of Tolstoi in French which my father had sent along and marked for my enjoyment and edification.

Edgar understood none of what I read, but my voice, speaking slowly and softly, my mouth a whisper away from his ear so that he could feel my intake and exhale of breath on his neck, made fine music. When the moon was high up we fished together for goldfish in our neighbor's pond, using large bent safety pins.

I told Edgar that now that he was more stocky in girth he reminded me of Napoleon. After Charlie Chaplin, Napoleon was my idle. In fact, I told him that I had written at age seventeen a piece for No. 4–5 of *Le Disque* published by Valéry Larbaud in Belgium, an essay titled "Charlie et Les Gosses" on both Napoleon and on my adored Charlie Chaplin. I took a pair of scissors and cut Edgar's hair into a short fringe like my impression of Napoleon. I showed him how to bend his hand across his chest and place it under his lapel à la Napoleon. I showed him how to pose and registered great laughter. He resembled Napoleon with the look in the eye of a wild horse and yet devoted and lovable as a great Dane.

Together we swam in the sea, plump, wearing nothing. Afterward I sang "You're the Cream in My Coffee" to him in four languages as we strolled through the town, so happy, until the sun set. We both agreed that the head-like mountain above the town had a profile from a distance like my father—forehead and all—as though he were watching over us. I put an ad in the newspaper for someone to come and teach us Chinese. We decided that Chinese would be the language of our home, as Italian had been the language of my childhood home. I wanted our children to speak Italian though also and one day I would teach it to Edgar in bed, word by word.

Our blissful holiday went on until it began to rain and the windows dripped night and day with large rolling drops. On a dark, dreary afternoon my buttered bread fell butter side down on the hearth. When Edgar retrieved it and saw that the butter was covered with ash and charcoal bits I started to weep. Edgar had never seen me weep and purposely threw his own bread down in the ash and charcoal so that I would not be alone in ruined buttered bread.

The coal bin was empty and Edgar insisted that he go into town for the night's supply. I said no to him with my wet eyes. He saw that I was shivering with chill and promised that he would quickly return with coal to keep us warm through the damp night. He was upset and spoke quickly to me in Greek, which I did not know. If only I had learned our Chinese, or had taught him Italian by then. I think he said that he would always love me.

I sank down into a chair. He placed a slide into my unwieldy ginger hair, which he found so lovable, and a blanket around my shoulders. He turned on the lamp, put his opera cape around his shoulders, before he shut the front door behind himself.

3 6

Father was told that the neighbors, smelling gas, had broken into the bungalow and found all the gas jets turned on at once. The entire room was painted black. An empty aspirin bottle lay on its side beside the blue bottle of Veronal, also empty. Fires were smoldering in the rug and in both my trunks.

I was found asleep in Kilmancanogue and made to drink mustard. Both sleeves of my coat were burning.

On 13 July I was taken to a *maison de santé* in Finglas. Aunt Eileen took time off from work and did what she could. Some of what had happened was kept out of the newspapers but several items appeared.

"Beware of torpor" were the words telegraphed to me by my father from Fontainebleau. "Je suis bien triste," he told Miss Weaver. He was suffering from insomnia and sympathetic hallucinations.

Aunt Eileen took me by boat to Holyhead and Miss Weaver took me the rest of the way back to England to her house, where all the windows but one were nailed shut. The one was nailed only halfway. When I began to throw Miss Weaver's books and papers out this half-opened window, it too was nailed shut. Before they could nail it, however, I threw out the white gossamer curtains, watching as they floated like ghosts slowly down to the ground, then, caught by a breeze, floated back up and into a tree.

A strong nurse named Edith Walker was hired to care

for me. For my dignity Miss Weaver asked her not to wear a nurse's uniform but I knew from the touch of her thumbs that she was a nurse. Then a second nurse was hired, then a third was needed. I had become as strong as a gorilla and was refusing to eat. Voices warned me night and day of approaching doom.

A five-week program of bovine-serum injections was prescribed by Dr. W. G. Macdonald, who was a surgeon but also a follower of Professor Ischlondsky's ideas. First Dr. Macdonald gave fifteen injections, then ten more. I fought like hell but lost the fight. Afterward Miss Weaver took me, now catatonic as an old dishrag, to Surrey to a small stone cottage for five months of total, enforced rest. A net hammock was tied between one oak and one ash tree. After breakfast the two nurses placed me in it and the third rocked me gently until lunch.

Father thought that perhaps a fur coat would help. Mother persuaded him to try a tweed coat this time. Father was being sued for £100 by the landlady in Bray: for broken furniture, burnt carpets, gas jets destroyed.

"Where are her two trunks of pretty clothes?" my mother kept inquiring.

3 7

Father sent me a camera as a gift. Between bouts of torpor I would sing to no one in either English, Italian, German, or French, at times in all four languages all mixed together. I went into manic singing contests with myself, songs from my whole song-infested life crowding at once into my mind.

When I could pull myself out of this "torpor" I would ask the nurses if it was true that my father had been reconciled with Ireland? Had Edgar and I achieved our goal? I was not sure. Trying to catch hold of a memory was like trying to pick a wet goldfish up into your hand from a pond. I'd think I had a grip on it, would start to close my fingers, and it would be too slippery and shoot away.

I tried repeatedly to write letters to my parents. Father wrote reams to me daily to cheer me on, pleading with me not to give up. I asked for young nettle tops to be mixed in with my food. I warned Miss Weaver and the nurses to wear gloves when picking them and to cut them with very sharp scissors. Before I'd go to sleep I'd make a line of empty milk bottles in front of my door so that I would be warned by hearing the glass break of any intruder's approaching to menace me in the dark.

When I closed my eyes at night I imagined my father as a young man wearing a nautical cap walking on spidery legs like a heron. My father had always bragged that lice would refuse to live on him, and in my sleep I imagined lice falling from trees onto my father's head as he brushed by waving his ashplant, but first falling on him and then dropping off, so that he left a trail of squirming live lice in his wake.

I saw a boy who had touched me in a private place when I was a little girl. I saw that boy now in my mind's eye, with stumps at the ends of his wrists as his hands had been removed.

Would I ever see the chestnut trees in Paris blooming again? Would Edgar return to me?

I asked to be put into a *maison de santé*. One was found one hundred miles from London.

They gave me tests.

I could not remain unless Father would certify me.

My father refused, and I was brought back to him and Mother in Paris.

3 8

It was March. The chestnuts were not in bloom.

After three weeks I was forcibly removed from the glat by two male nurses, who first encased me in a *camisole de force*.

They took me to Le Vésinel, a clinic, and in April to the Delmas Clinic in Ivry, just outside of Paris.

Now the doctors diagnosed me as having "cyclothymia." The previous diagnosis of "dementia praecox" was abandoned. My mother did not visit me anymore because I was a dager to her. Was this hard or easy for her, I would like to know?

Father came to visit every Sunday, repeating over and over, "You will get well. You will get well. Yes, you will get well."

39

In 1936, while I was still at Ivry, Father presented me
with a beautifully bound edition of his work, which had
used my finely drawn and colored *lettrines* as illustrations.
He included a copy of *Revue des Deux Mondes*, in which an
art critic had mentioned my illustrations. This gift was
meant to remind me of my many dormant but not atro-
phied talents. Ha.

Insulin treatments were tried.

V I

At Thirty

The Story of the Blotting-Paper
Girl (Keep Them Guessing for
Three Hundred Years)—Continued

A Memoir by Lucia Joyce

40

*F*ATHER never missed a visit, even after I shouted at him, "Che bello! Che bello!" and wrapped my hands around his neck and squeezed until a strong nurse pulled me away.

For the next four years Father's theory was that the real root of all of my misadventures and wretchedness was infections of various degrees through the years in my teeth.

Despite a hefty nurse lurking always near us, Father and
I played the piano together each Sunday, sang together, ate
Italian cakes together. He taught me Latin for myself, and
Greek to speak to Edgar when he returned. As his eyes
worsened Mother arranged each week for a friend, or
sometimes Giorgio, to guide him to Ivry, and to wait over
coffee or whiskey in the café down the road while Father
made his visit.

He returned home each Sunday very low spirited and
silent indeed. During the entire afternoon and night
mother could not get him to eat or speak or work.

Nevertheless, before 1938 had concluded, Father sat
quite immobile on a bench on a quiet street of Paris. He
did not know if he could find the strength to stand up ever
again. Every muscle and sinew had gone slack. He could
see nothing through his useless eyes but dancing specks of
white light with the left and the pale mauve shadow of two
trees with his right.

He had completed the book he had worked on night
and day for seventeen years.

He was not to riot again and I never knew why.

4 1

At Delmas a moment became a day which became a
year. Or was it a week?

It was France? It was Italy? It was Plyme? A four-year-
old Lucia conjured up Giorgio, calling him Faustino, her
brother, her ellipsis, a lightning rod.

Faustino lashed in the eye by the end of a cabman's whip when in a fury the cabman beat his horse. Faustino with little glinting rimless glasses. Faustino, distraught because Father initialed his books, made other marks as well, and Faustino shouted, "I will inherit these books upon your death. They will be mutilated."

Father insisted that Faustino sing tenor parts. "But you are a baritone," his teachers told him.

Faustino acting as a lightning rod during thunder and lightning storms feared by Mother, Father, and me.

Faustino and I speaking Italian in France. Faustino wanting to study medicine but not knowing French. Faustino over six feet tall by age sixteen. I determined not to stop growing until I was the same height. I stopped before. Faustino a dandy; groomed, cleaned, combed, scrubbed to a point of pinkness. His friends in Trieste whispered that his father—goat's beard and all—resembled the devil. His friends in Zürich called his father "Herr Satan."

Faustino wanting to take care of horses. Mocked by father.

Faustino beginning his professional singing career. An enemy of Father's calling him Archie. Faustino publicly condemning Father's wine drinking, ignoring his own drinking of whiskey to the point of melting. Faustino was put two years behind me in school in Zürich during the Great War. Faustino called by his Uncle "Deasil" a melomaniac.

When reprimanded by our parents I sobbed and Faustino sulked. He had raised the practice of sulking to an art form. Faustino sulked through an entire holiday in Lausanne. His eyes looked lavender to me, big as a cow's through his glasses when I saw him lean over to look at me, fall forward, his spectacles piercing my chin. Almost my very first memory.

Faustino belonged to our mother. I belonged to our father.

Faustino was coming tomorrow to take me home with him. Or. We had been left together at home while our parents went to the opera?

Faustino would find the singing mockingbird.

My many doctors and nurses at Delmas, opaque and odorless to me, heard not the voices shouting at me, but heard me shout in four languages, asking for help, and could see waves of terror breaking against my face and hands. "Don't shout," I begged them. "When I don't reply to you it is not because I am deaf."

Mother and Faustino. Father's hand on my blue-veined wrist.

The black derby hat was not permitted to be delivered to my room because I was under heavy sedation, restrained and under observation night and day to protect me from my own hands tearing open my own throat.

4 2

Father sent the tall beanpole, Mr. Beckett, in search of E. A. Father and Oblomov had reconciled. Mr. Beckett sent in his report to Father each evening time, before his walk, by telephone. "Ségur quatre-vingt-quinze-vingt," he would tell the operator, "Ségur 95-20."

E. A. was not to be found.

Mr. Beckett had been enlisted to supervise the typing and proofing of Father's new manuscript with the hope that he could interrupt Father's frightful bad luck with typists and proofs.

Some examples. An English typist had once obliterated forty-odd pages of an earlier manuscript, which, he had decided, was pornography. Another had arrived at Father's flat with her pages, thrown them on the floor, spat on them, stepped on them, and left making shhhhing noises. Still another's husband had thrown what he considered to be filth into the fire. The wife smuggled what she had been able to pull from the fire, charred, back to Father. One particularly vivid episode of his early book had been shunned by eight typists, the ninth had been stopped before he'd been able to throw it out the window across the rooftops of Paris.

I'd call that bad luck. Secretaries too were problems.

A total of three secretaries had been injured in some way or other after they had worked for Father. One helper had inserted punctuation, another had inserted red notations into the place for purple, green into the place for blue, and yellow also into the green.

The trouble seemed to have been started by Father himself when, in 1911, Mother had got out of bed when he wished her please to stay in bed. He stormed up himself and tossed his first book in manuscript form into the stove. Because his sister Eileen was visiting from Ireland at the time and happened to see the melodrama, she reached inside the stove barehanded and, scalding her palm, grabbed back the thick bundle of typescript, putting it under her mattress until her brother came back to his senses. When he did, she presented the work to him baked into a bread, which he discovered when he tried to slice it. He was overjoyed, tears fell, and, as a gift, he presented her with his only silk scarf—blue and white dots.

Mr. Beckett had once also accidentally joined in the fiasco. While taking dictation from Father, he heard a songbird at the window singing, then a knock at the door. Father said, *"Come in."*

Mr. Beckett had written what was said. When they went over the day's work and Mr. Beckett read in the text, "Come in," Father stopped him and asked if he'd said those words. Mr. Beckett told Father he had. Loving coincidence as he did, Father decided, "Let it stand!" and it did.

Mr. Beckett painstakingly typed the oftimes illegible book and then helped Father, magnifying glass in hand, slowly, carefully, to correct the proofs.

That is, until Mr. Beckett, one night on the avenue d'Orléans, was stabbed by a pimp named Prudent. As he bled, the knife still stuck in his pleura, a piano student, Suzanne Deschevaux-Dumesnil, rode by on her bicycle, saw Beckett, and called an ambulance. He was taken to Hôpital Broussair, Verlaine's hospital.

Mother sent him a custard pudding. Taking bits and pieces from several of the eighteen languages and modern tongues that he had used to construct his ambiguous work, Father wrote Mr. Beckett a long, buoying letter on rhubarb, the leaf blade of which could cause death.

In return, Mr. Beckett penned a short epistle on the rhododendron, an ornamental plant capable of causing death.

Father visited Mr. Beckett in hospital, bringing the *Irish Times*. From his hospital bed, Mr. Beckett read aloud, as he had done in Father's flat late in the afternoon, all the news from the *Irish Times* to Father, who looked off at the ceiling, head cocked, as he listened. Father had arranged a private room for Mr. Beckett for this purpose. In keeping with the morbid atmosphere, Father described his twenty-six eye operations to Mr. Beckett and the day in 1923 when, while he was still conscious, seventeen infected teeth had been removed at one time.

If a chill penetrated the afternoon air, Father refolded the *Irish Times* and adjusted it against his lower back and kidneys beneath his jacket as a second vest against the cold night air. "Je suis vide," he told Mr. Beckett.

Mr. Beckett did not dispute this. Mr. Beckett could hear the receding sound of Father whistling "None but the Lonely Heart" as he made his way home to Mother feeling along the walls as he walked.

Bored by convalescence, Mr. Beckett resumed his searching for Edgar after he had been released. Father counseled him, as I had instructed, to look for Napoleon. In fact, better yet, Father advised to find a comfortable place to perch and simply scan, as Edgar himself would be searching for me and would eventually canvass the whole of Paris, inevitably passing any place that Mr. Beckett chose to read.

Mr. Beckett chose the quarter of St. Denis to wait. A

perfect pink pearl arrived in the mail for me. The next day
a perfect gray pearl arrived.

Mr. Beckett saw a white-and-gold Rolls-Royce drive by
with a live cheetah sitting upright in the back seat. He saw
a black bear being pulled by a rope attached to a ring
through its nose by a very young Gypsy boy with no shoes
on his almost black feet.

Keeping on the lookout for E. A. suited Mr. Beckett's
solitary temperament. Besides amateurish flute playing
and plans for suicide at night, helping Father—reading
aloud, running errands, dictation, typing—in the afternoon and early evening, his life was free of any obliga-
tions. Since he had spurned me in 1930 and had been
exiled by Father for more than four years, idolizing Father
as he did he was eager to satisfy Father's every need now
that he was back in his good graces.

Mr. Beckett's morbid temperament matched Father's
mood of despair. Though Father was convinced without
a doubt that I would most certainly recover, perhaps, he
thought, when he was no longer an inhabitant of this
earth, I would at last be released. Mr. Beckett had heard
that the great Nijinsky had been relieved of his curse by
insulin injections and told this to Father. Father daily
awaited news that I had been transformed as well; would
be freed to relieve my parents' immense suffering and
guilt.

Both Irishmen steeped their silences like very strong
tea; their silences ranged in atmosphere from wistful to
dirgelike. Both men looked elsewhere when spoken to and
always behaved with excessive cordiality. In spite of po-

liteness, Father did not think Mr. Beckett a suitable match
for me. Neither did Mother. Neither did I, remembering
his past dismissal of me and that in a book called *More
Kicks Than Pricks* Mr. Beckett had used my name almost,
Lucie, for a crippled girl.

Now that E. A. had got caught in my throat, I didn't
care.

Mr. Beckett saw a small dark man repeatedly drive
through his quarter of Paris in a canary-yellow Hispano-
Suiza motorcar. Each time the car reappeared a different
exotic woman sat beside the intense, black-eyed driver.
Meticulously drawn on the door of the motorcar, a hammer and sickle.

Mr. Beckett observed a Red Cross team of white-hatted
sisters canvassing the neighborhood for donations to send
to the West China victims of drought, five million or
more of whom had already entered immortality.

Mr. Beckett agreed with Father that motorcars should
be forbidden in cities. Motoring brought out unpleasant
arrogances in their passengers and drivers; they were a
menace to pedestrians. Taxis, streetcars, horses, and bicy-
cles were ample.

Mr. Beckett saw a very fat woman with a man's haircut
wearing a brown velvet hat walking a large black dog. Mud
was sprayed on him by a passing taxi. A family of pathetic
refugees repeatedly asked him questions in an indecipher-
able language. Pus poured from the ears of the refugees'
grubby children.

4 3

Father and Mother moved to rue des Vignes.

In what seemed like slow motion Mother set fire to letter after letter until none remained from a packet she had kept for almost thirty years wrapped in a flannel nightgown always in her lingerie drawer. She thought two thoughts, first—"Jim, there is one who understands you," and second, "Shouldn't there have been more of these?"

A small, perfectly formed green parakeet perched on the sill of the open window. The bird was intent on the curling fumes and fakes of carbon left after the fames had rolled across the length of the letter.

Mother jumped, but the bird did not move. She called out, "Jim!"

Responding to the tone of her voice and holding on to the backs of the furniture, he felt his way until he'd touched his wife's creamy neck. Because of his bad eyes, the bird seemed to him to be an iridescent pale green spot but, knowing Mother as well as he did, and the sound of her voice still reverberating in his mind, he heard a dim chirp, wiped the point of his pen on his elbow, replaced its cover and hooked it onto his pocket, took up the tin oval wastebasket as a net, and captured the soft green spot while causing a snowstorm of charred, carbonized paper to swirl across his own face and Mother's thick still *rousse* auburn hair.

He held the soft parakeet in his hand.

He sent Mr. Beckett for a cage of wife. Father had been

reading Sean O'Faolain's *Bird Alone*. The coincidence caused him to feel an infusion of hope.

Shortly thereafter a second parakeet came into their lives, Laufawwn. Father united the pair in the cage. The pair were named Pierre and Pipi.

44

For my birthday in 1939 my parents visited Ivry. The looming war cast a most ominous shadow across all of Paris, Ivry, France. I was thirty-two years old and could see nothing but the scar on my chin as the sum total of my thirty-two years, my unmarried status, a failure as an artist as well, a rocking chair that had kept rocking after I got up.

I was to be moved down to Brittany to La Baule, where the entire Hotel Edelweiss would be turned into a *maison de santé*. Taking Pierre along, Mother and Father made the journey to La Baule to wait for my arrival, as the political ferment all around them—besides diverting attention from Father's new book—was pressing against one and all. They feared especially for me with nothing and no one to brace myself against. Rooms were hard to find as the flood of refugees increased daily.

The *maison* was moved to Pornichet near La Baule instead.

War was declared.

Father banged on the doctor's door with the top of his

cane. Splinters of wood flew. "Lucia must not be abandoned in terror if bombardment comes to Brittany!"

In a frenzy of terror I begged my parents to stay with me.

Father and Mother gave me Pierre for company. Still more refugees crowded the hotels and streets.

One night my parents ate a silent dinner at a very large restaurant. Mother coaxed Father to eat his untouched food. Mother did not know that while she dressed, as he had been doing every night of late, he had sneaked into the back door of a café and quickly drunk four strong whiskeys, which was killing even his usual minuscule appetite. She coaxed to no avail. A throng of French and English soldiers suddenly filled the place to bursting, hundreds of young, tender pink faces with shining hair wearing fresh uniforms.

Together they began to sing the "Marseillaise."

Tremulously, with the Irish tenor voice that had been likened favorably to John McCormack's in his youth, Father joined in.

The sweetness and fineness of his voice stood out and all three hundred soldiers grew silent. Three hundred pairs of eyes bore into him. Liquid tenderness lapped against all pairs of ears.

Two soldiers lifted Father up onto a zinc table, and all listened attentively while he sang the song again. All verses, slowly. Together once more they all sang as though with one voice, with the timbre of immediate victory swelling up their voices. The atmosphere of invulnerability buoyed all of them.

Germany beware!

Hysterical telephone calls from Giorgio overwhelmed them. Because Giorgio was in a crisis, Mother and Father decided to return to Paris.

Father swore to me, "We will shortly return."

I was beside myself with panic. "Stay with me," I pleaded.

"We'll return shortly," he assured and reassured me as well as he could, as my state was similar to a cyclone. "Giorgio needs us."

Three strong nurses gripped me at my shoulders and hips. Father's glasses glinted in the morning light, as though coded signals were being flashed first on the ceiling, then on the wall, on the ceiling, on the nurse's breast, on my throat. I tried to catch the signals from my father in my hands to decode. To have my eyes licked open like a new calf by my mother's wet tongue would have helped. I needed seeing eyes and free hands to decode but my eyes were swimming and my arms were in vice.

I tasted salt on my lips.

I saw their straight backs. I saw a thick chain encircling my father's ankle, attached to my mother's wrist. The key to the chain, a long, thin gold latchkey, had nestled for thirty-five years in my mother's esophagus, where she had, forced by her husband, swallowed it in 1912. I could see a slight yellow glow where the gold lodged and glowed through her body like a key-shaped question mark.

"We will return, Lucia," I heard my father's goive. "You'll not be left alone."

My father's voice was a soft feather across my cheeks

and lips. His wife had every right to hate me. Had my parents' spines been fused by God?

"I'll wait for you," I tried to say but could not tell if it had come out in words or between the words.

It was Pierre and I, at the mercy of the mighty German. Shortly the much-feared bombardments began at Pornichet.

I never saw either of my parents again and wait for them to this very day.

4 5

My parents moved from rue des Vignes to boulevard Raspail, the Hôtel Lutétia. Father left almost everything behind at rue des Vignes. Father was drinking to great excess, spending money wildly and foolishly, and instigating fallings-out with his dearest friends. His son's life was kaput.

"The last Christmas is coming," he told Mr. Beckett.

It came and went for them but not for me.

Then in St. Gérand-le-Puy, at the Hôtel de la Paix with friends, Father was doubled over by excruciating pain in his clavier.

When the pain had abated, cane in hand, dark glasses on, and long, black winter overcoat reaching almost into the dust, he walked, tapping his cane to feel his way, nund and nund and back again through the small, dull village.

A lifelong dog hater, dog fearer, he gathered a pocketful

of pebbles and rocks before beginning his daily walk.
Between the stones and his walking stick, he was ready to
encounter the village population of mangy, rude dogs.

"Our dogs are not dangerous," an offended villager
told him after watching a barrage of stones fly at a village
dog.

"All dogs have no souls," Father responded, walking
on.

Besides sitting silently in the back of the local church in
a straight-backed chair to hear the music, he wrote lengthy
letters to me and to the administrative head of my *maison
de santé*, giving instructions for my comfort and protection when the much-feared bombings occurred. He read
Goethe's *Conversation with Eckermann* slowly and with
difficulty because of so little sight in his eyes. St. Lucia was
the patron saint of eyesight. What good had I done? None.

Mr. Beckett visited by train to deliver his report of total
failure. He had discovered no sign whatsoever of E. A.
anywhere in grim Paris. "Persevere," Father told Mr.
Beckett. "I know in my heart that Mr. Anthagros will not
fail his Lucia. He has given his word long ago to me."

Had not Holland, Denmark, Belgium, and Norway
fallen to the Germans, and finally Paris on 14 June, I might
have succeeded in being transferred to Moulin. Father had
been finalizing arrangements for me from Vichy, where he
had gone for that purpose and to get away from the dogs.

Father's funds were blocked.

Mr. Beckett had no source of funds.

Perhaps he could find a way to bring me to Kilchberg
near to Zürich? My whole family could be near to me in

Zürich. They'd taken refuge from the last war in Zürich. This time it seemed like an almost impossible feat to arrange. Father was sure that he had waited much too long.

46

Father had long ago predicted of France: "In a year France will be Fascist. But there is reason to believe that she will not have to call in fascism from the outside, it will come to her from within."

Italian entry into the war on 10 June had especially pained him, proving him wrong as well, as he still had a soft spot for Italian opera, language, Italian attitude toward life. "The Italians are capable of a great deal of foolishness but of little harm," he had said about them. He had always believed that the only menacing thing about Italy was the fierce and wild north Adriatic bora wind, which had often flung him and other Triestines against walls and each other.

When he was a boy Father was thrashed by his fellow students after school. The students had elected Tennyson as the best poet. Father had insisted that Byron was better. After the thrashing they asked him again, "Who is the better poet?"

"Byron without a doubt," he had replied.

So they had thrashed him again.

His tenacity was undiminished despite the condition of

his thwarted spirit and the bad health plaguing him. He had always thought of himself as apart from history, standing off to the side, paring his nails. History, he saw, had not seen him this way and had swept him along with no special consideration.

His first plan began to cohere around Bern and the Maison de Santé Pré Carré near Chavornay.

On 4 August the insurmountable was surmounted when the German authority issued a *permis de sortie* for me.

Then the plan fell through.

Despair again was rampant until, heartened by a chance hearing on a radio inside a local café playing "Lebendig Begraben" written by a friend and sung movingly by Felix Lifford, Father again focused on the plan for Zürich.

The needed elements again began to cohere: money, guarantees, massive paperwork, all shuffled into the correct order.

Then. Boom. Blank walls.

47

Miss Weaver later told me that, although warned by Father to stay away from Paris, Paul Léon, the former Jew of Russian origin who had long ago converted to Catholicism, climbed through a window at rue des Vignes in an effort to retrieve personal papers, some of an "intimate" nature, to return to Father.

The Germans had begun hounding and arresting Jews in France. Despite his conversion to Catholicism, he was considered to be thoroughly Jewish by the Germans.

Mr. Beckett saw him in Paris and told him that he must leave immediately.

Painstakingly, this true friend catalogued and assembled Father's papers and deposited them with the neutral Irish consul with instructions (I read in one of my father's biographies) to return papers to James Joyce in the unlikely case of his own death, or give them to the Irish library in the even more unlikely event of both their deaths, but only after a fifty-year seal had been placed on them, a time only the curious would live to see.

At this point Mr. Beckett further entreated him to get out of Paris. I would have done the same.

More loyalties intervened. First Mr. Léon bought at auction possessions of Father's being sold by his landlord in lots in big baskets in lieu of unpaid rent. Most people were more interested in pots and chairs, so he shrewdly bought back things that were of real value to Father and stored them in his own home to return to Father after the war. Second, he stayed on in order to offer support to his own son in school examinations.

That very night a knock was heard at his door. Though he had long ago converted, the Gestapo arrested him, deported him to the camp close to Compiègne designed for Jews and others as a holding place until they could be sorted and shipped elsewhere.

After one and a half years' imprisonment in Silesia, this friend was shot to death.

4 8

Insurmountable obstacles to departure from France:

Funds to pay off what were owed for my incarceration in Pornichet.

The Swiss announce that father is a Jew.

Expired passports.

Expired *permis de sortie.*

Twenty thousand Swiss francs wanted in a Swiss bank as a guarantee.

Permission for Giorgio but not for me.

Permission for me but not for Giorgio.

Then permission for Giorgio but not for me.

It was forbidden for foreigners to go to Vichy; arrest would result. All legal maneuvers must be done in Vichy.

Refusals.

Refusal to ask for Irish passports.

Refusal to go to America.

It was decided. They would leave with Giorgio, in hourly anger of conscription into the army. They would have to arrange for me to join them from the safety of neutral Swiss soil.

Father was experiencing grave stomach pain and was almost blind. Mother could barely walk, sit, or stand because of arthritis. Giorgio wasn't afraid of the Germans.

Nonetheless, as they boarded the 3 A.M. train with darkened windows from St. Germain-des-Fossés on 14 December 1940, the genius who had been singled out by a critic for his "gli acustissimi occhi" put his back to France. For twenty years in France he had lived at seventeen addresses. When the train began to move he kept this "gli acustissimi occhi"[6] always focused at Pornichet on me.

49

Father's special shade of green ink had spilled through all the layers of their clothes in their suitcase. A stain in the shape of a two-headed bird decorated every item of clothing.

As though I were there beside him in the flesh, my clairvoyance saw him in Geneva. He immediately went to explore a *maison de santé* close to Chavornet for me. (Not a bad one, but he didn't like it.) Then by train they went on to Zürich to Hôtel Pension Delphin, oblivious of the green two-headed-bird stain on the front of his shirt and the back of her dress.

The weather was dreary, snow with rain. Paul Ruggiero visited them at the Pension Delphin on Mühlebachstrasse, the street on which Father had walked me to school when I was seven years old. Mr. Ruggiero set his hat on the bed. I tried to warn him but he did not heed me.

Father swooped down to grab it off the bed but it had already settled. The superstition was that a death would occur. "Someone will die," he told Mother and their friend.

Mr. Ruggiero reached for the hat to remove it.

"It doesn't matter now," Father told him. "Let it stay."

Father and Giorgio sang together in Latin and Irish and

listened to "A Moon of My Delight," sung by John McCormack with much pleasure. Father took long strolls alone in the wet snow beside the lake. He caught Mother by the coat when she slipped on some icy steps when leaving a restaurant. "Why can't we ever stay at home?" she snapped at him.

Father was stricken with pain again. He was taken by emergency ambulance to Roten Kreuz Hospital.

Blood transfusion was necessary. Young Swiss soldiers volunteered. They were from Neufchâtel, the area that gave the name to his favorite white wine. Even in his semiconscious condition this gave him hope; was a good omen. Through his fog he saw that one of the soldiers was an almost spitting image of a young Napoleon. He made a mental note to write this to me.

His greatest fear besides thunder and dogs was of going unconscious. He asked Mother to leep beside him as he had done with her when she had been in hospital many years before, and she had done with him the times of his many eye operations. In thirty-seven years of their life together they had only been separated a handful of nights.

The doctor urged her to go back to the hotel o sleep. She did and when Father came out of his greatly dreaded unconscious state, he saw that she was not there. He did not know that I was there instead.

He called, "Nora!"

She was summoned but he died before he could look at her Irish face one last time.

Mother had a special wreath made in the shape of a lyre.

The tenor Max Meili sang *"Addio terra, addio cielo."*

Giorgio held on to Mother's arm.

I was informed but was unbelieving. "Just like him," I explained, "to spy on us from under the earth. Be mindful, he'll return. You'll see, he'll awake."

Remember, I was there!

From his grave in Zürich, close to the famous zoological gardens, the roar of the great lion could often be heard night and day. So say all the biographies. They do not know that the lion roars at an empty hole in the ground.

Father was supposed to have died on the 13th of January. His mother had died on the number 13 as well, but in August. There was that number 13! Luckily he hadn't really died, he'd be able to explain it all to me, I was sure—where he really did go—and we'd have a laugh, the great lion's roar and all.

5 0

"He's about as sincere as a jellyfish; as an ironing board," I said about my doctor to Pierre.

Being a Jew, Pierre had been made to wear a yellow star.

Blackouts became common. Often in the dark I saw blue-and-white-check carpet slippers shuffle toward me. A ring-encrusted hand would reach out of the darkness patting the air or wall; the hand would corkscrew into the dark and would straighten its spectacles, sending a gleam of recognition out into the room. For an instant I would glimpse a bulging forehead; Brayhead still watching me.

Sometimes the ring-encrusted hand dipped inside a dark velvet jacket, exposing hunting scenes embroidered into the tapestry wool vest. The half-lit head, a jaunty hat perched atop, seemed to be looking at me and then turning away into the gloom.

I heard Mother snap at me, "Butterfingers!"

I saw chairs flying.

I wished I could find my copy of *Vita Nuova* by Dante that my father had given to me, but it had been mislaid somewhere in other places I had been but I couldn't remember the names of these places. Now they told me there was a war.

"If he is really dead," I whispered to Pierre, "he will never again eat chocolates out of his own cricket cap. None of us will again eat Bar-le-Duc jellies, or Montargies pralines, or get together to play Forfeits or sing 'It's a Long Way to Tipperary.'"

I knew he was not dead. He had lit a candle for me on 13 December. I had seen it, Mother had not.

Both Pierre and I had promised each other to die before falling into German hands. We had heard that Christians were being offered rewards of a half kilogram of salt for each Jew, either dead or alive. "What for?" I asked.

"If only I'd buried eggs in a potato field," I announced with regret.

The *maison* still had ample food to eat. One very mean doctor ordered me kept tied to my own bed, which was nailed to the floor.

5 1

Rain came drumming and tapping on the thick glass windowpane bringing information. A great ledger sheet was laid out across Europe. If the writing hadn't been so thick I would have been able to calculate the debits and to predict what was to come. Approaching winter brought more rain, and wind made the trees groan and cry all night.

"Why are my eyes so small and close together?" I asked my doctor. "If my nose was larger, none of this would have happened," I told him.

As a refugee, Pierre was deprived of his nationality, becoming a stateless Jew under the new Statut des Juifs. He was subject to internment in a "shelter camp."

At four in the morning he was arrested and taken to Vélodrôme d'Hiver with thousands of others, where ten latrines and one street hydrant for water were all that had been provided for everyone to use. The place was rife with diphtheria, scarlet fever, measles, vermin. Pierre's few French francs were taken away and Polish zlotys were returned to him in their place.

Pierre saw children separated from their parents. He was grouped with the children. Like the other children who became uncontrollably hysterical when they were being led to trains, he too had to be forcibly carried, wings flapping and screaming in fear, by the gendarmes, and locked inside a freight train meant for cattle and not people.

When these boxcars returned to their starting point in occupied Belgium, the railwaymen opened the sliding doors, the sunlight pouring inside the dark cars, twenty-five small bodies between the ages of two and four years old lay in the straw. Blinded by thirst and the bright light, Pierre flew with his remaining strength toward this light, high as he could go, feeling greasy hair brush against his feathers.

5 2

In Pornichet bombardments began. Louder than the loudest thunder, making the earth shake. I lost all track of dark or light and what year it was. I remembered how desperately my mother had prayed out loud while we rowed together, singing together, on Locarno Lake, when a sudden lightning-and-thunder storm had turned the sky black and then sent veins of gold through the dark and terror so wild through my mother's *rousse* hair that prayer had tumbled from her mouth.

I knew no prayer but, in a ferocious vice that sounded like my own mother's, screamed, "Cat mara agus marbh-fháisc uirthi!"[7]

"Guíodóireacht! Seargú!"[8]

The bombardment, like thunderclaps, became so constant that I couldn't tell where I left off and the war began. Cold sores covered my lips.

Between bombardments I couldn't taste my food.

5 3

My clairvoyance told me that it was the box filled with coal and not the frayed opera cape that brought E. A. to the attention of the police outside of Pornichet not seven miles from one who whispered his name between deliriums of terror and loss of all muscle control. A policeman with an empty coal stove at home took the coal and Edgar was put with a convoy of men between sixteen and forty-five recently rounded up for a forced-labor brigade.

Edgar and four others were sent to Drancy to service empty cattle cars, which smelled worse than a whole cellar of onions that had rotted so much that they were black.

They were given such bad food that he and his mates trapped and ate sparrows.

5 4

Then he and many others were sent to a place called Oswiecim.

There an officer with a stone instead of a face made Edgar wear a white armband over his coat. On it was written in black letters: BLÖD.[9]

His costume in the opera, stripes. The spotlights were

much brighter than *Guillaume Tell.* Going and coming
each day in wooden, mismatched shoes that stuck in the
mud, an orchestra played sentimental German songs,
Bach also. The sirens heightened the music. Electric
sparks flew from a wire fence, which had charred areas
with what looked like parts of dead animals still stuck.

5 5

As the scenes progressed Edgar recalled that in Genti
Couli when a child had mumps his cheeks were painted
with either a red or a blue Star of David. Here there were
red triangles, lavender triangles, red and yellow stars, and
yellow stripes sewn on the clothes. It seemed like no two
people spoke the same language.

No water except in soup. E. A. conjured up how the
children in his village fathered together to make rain.
Some carried old shoes while a procession went through
all the narrow streets and then down to the harbor, singing
repeatedly:

> *Water, O God, that the earth needs.*
> *Children, children and infants,*
> *We need bread, but we have no water.*
> *Open the skies and drench our fields.*
> *God, God, throw wheat in abundance.*
> *Amen!*

And another song:

> *Before me is an angel that looks at me.*
> *I want to speak and cannot, my heart is sighing.*
>
> *I return and say, what is to become of me?*
> *I do not want to die in a strange country.*
> *I return and say, what is to become of me?*
> *I do not want to die in a strange country.*
> *The city is on fire and no one to put it out.*

5 6

On 6 September 1944 in the morning were heard unusual explosions.

The lightning of the beacon at the top of the Swiss Alps had been the signal that the people's uprising had begun. Guillaume Tell would be saved. What would be the signal in this opera, that the end was at last coming for all of them? For me?

5 7

Snow fell. The whine of bombers came down from the sky. Smoke filled the air night and day from the crematoria chimneys. The raw wind from the Carpathians no longer froze him; he felt neither cold nor hunger nor curiosity any longer.

5 8

In his stupor, almost dead, he heard the clanking of a cow bell; he saw himself chasing a goat through the streets of Paris. A chicken with my face jumped from a passing train window, flapped along the snowy ground toward him, then clucked and strutted against him, pecking his fingertips, which hung down like bones.

I set a meal before him. A bowl of hot broth with lazy steamlike mist rising, a roasted goose, brown, tender, juicy, crackling. I called to him. He didn't know what language I was speaking. "Salato. Salz. Sal. Chiste. Sel."

He repeated my words. "Saluto. Salz. Sal. Chiste. Sel."

I placed a small chunk of rock on his tongue.

His glands ached painfully at the taste of salt.

5 9

The opera ended when men wearing dirty fur flickered in the distance emerging from the snow, appearing to be wolves, and, on getting closer, spoke in the Russian language. The Russian nurses carried grown men in their arms like small children through trails of human diarrhea frozen into the snow.

In Pornichet I spat on anyone who tried to put their hands on me. I was helpless to stop the rocking chairs rocking, but by the time the opera was over, my knees were stiff. Waiting, basting, *la ruche!* Kinch. "A una fonte afflitta."

6 0

E. A. saw the sun rise on the mountains of Lavrion from the deck of a ship. He saw his fellow passengers weep.

6 1

Rst, wide open to allow the cool breeze to enter.

He looked in and saw his own mother, now transformed into a very, very old lady, rinsing salt off a plucked and headless chicken.

6 2

Edgar was made by his mother to wear a bag around his waist. It contained feathers, pulverized lizard eggs, talcum, the hair of a jackass. It was her wish before she died, which she expected to do very soon, that her beloved son, her only surviving blood relation, marry as quickly as possible so her old eyes could have one glimpse of his child before they closed for good; that a single remnant of their obliterated family would live on. Even the tombstones of the Jewish cemetery had been ripped apart and aken to sreve as latrine linings. It was possible to see a tombstone embedded with other stones along the uneven road having been used to page these roads. There all the ancestors had been strewn, or had been last seen after being ordered to register and assemble in Liberty Square for forced-labor brigades or emigration to Waldsee.

No one else but Edgar had gone away and ever returned. Praise be to God!

She took hairs from every part of his body to put on a girl's doorstep.

She was sure his mind had become deranged when he tried to explain to her all the things his own eyes had seen before, during and after Waldsee. She knew such things could not have taken place on earth. It was impossible.

She grew impatient when he told her of a mermaid with whom he had fallen in love and whom he had sworn to protect. Always in a cold sweat he tried to explain, growing shaky as he talked, that she was in France. "I can take the hairs there and put them on her doorstep!"

At these words his mother would turn her face away from him, put her hag's hand on her heart, and moan, "My heart. I'm getting a heart attack!"

VII

At Seventy

NURSE LEARY retired in 1977 at the age of sixty-five. Her departure coincided with Lucia's transfer to the geriatric section of the hospital, St. Monica's Ward. Before she left, Lucia asked her to put an ad in the newspaper and please ask scholars and biographers to stop calling on her. She was too tired and fed up with the past to help them. "It's a heart-pilfering experience," Lucia explained.

After Mrs. Leary's difficult departure, Miss Joyce wrote often to her and sometimes included letters she had received from Mr. Beckett and others to make a point. Lucia missed her terribly; after all she had seen her nearly every day for almost half her life.

More than ever now she looked forward to Miss Lidderdale's visits. Over the years since Miss Weaver's death, Miss Lidderdale had come regularly and could always find some way to make Lucia laugh. She was a great joke maker.

She took Lucia to shop for clothes and Lucia could not understand why the shopgirl would guide her to the large ladies' sizes. Several times Miss Lidderdale took Lucia for drives in a hired car. They visited churches way out in the country and Miss Lidderdale allowed her a glass of amber sherry before lunch. She even saw some children from the car but could not touch them as the car was in motion.

During her many visits, though, Miss Lidderdale never mentioned her famous father, had gotten to know her, and seemed to like her only for herself and not for her father's greatness.

Lucia hoped that Miss Lidderdale would never find out about her famous father. She liked someone loving her just for herself. Could it really be possible?

She didn't like, though, the way that Miss Lidderdale kept encouraging her to go up to the art department to draw.

"I'm too lazy," she admitted. "It's hundreds of yards away, up a long flight of steps. You know I don't cooperate up there. Can't we just sit here and smoke? You know how much I like to smoke. Make me laugh again, Miss Lidderdale! Remember, if my parents come for a visit, I wouldn't want to miss them."

For Christmas Mrs. Leary brought Lucia an old fur wrap that had belonged to her mother-in-law. The mother-in-law had died the year before and left her worldly goods and £500 saved over her entire lifetime to her eldest son, who was not Mr. Leary. Mrs. Leary hadn't expected much, but she had hoped for a small annuity to help make ends meet and not a ratty fur wrap; prices were always climbing and now, with both of them retired, their pensions remained the same. Perhaps they would never be able to put in central heating.

Lucia paraded up and down the halls in her new fur wrap. In uncharacteristic effusion she kissed Mrs. Leary three times on her cheeks. Mrs. Leary turned red.

"Look at you, sister," Lucia commented. "After three decades of chatter, you're dumb as an oyster now."

Pleased, Nurse Leary turned to go. Lucia quietly added after her, "Never fear, sister, I'll never tell where you keep your hand at night. But do mind yourself when motoring on narrow lanes," she warned, the back of Mrs. Leary's head receding down the long corridor because she had not heard what Lucia was saying.

As she had done alone in 1951 to meet Miss Joyce coming from France, in 1978 she and her husband Jim took the boat train to England. She brought with them a small overnight case and he carried two shirt boxes wrapped with brown paper and tied up with string. She didn't dare ask what they were. They checked into the Euston Hotel, not wanting to stray far from the Euston station area. He told her he had some business to take care of on the other side of town As he was too timid to take a taxi, she purchased a street map in the hotel kiosk so that he could walk the entire way to his destination, the shirt boxes under his arm.

While she waited for him she counted the rooms in the hotel. She counted seven hundred thirty-two. She went down and had a second breakfast with Danish bacon, New Zealand butter on Dutch toast, and English tea. She felt the way Miss Joyce must have in her traveling days.

Then she walked into the street, took a long stroll, and found a fun arcade in Piccadilly. She changed an English pound note into twopence pieces and played on a machine that had slots that took twopence pieces in and ran them out onto a platform of similar coins arranged in piles trembling along a ledge. When the recently inserted copper met the moving platform of coins, which seemed as though it would easily topple, it sometimes actually would topple, sending coins cascading down a chute into her hands. Perhaps every second time she played the game she would hear the coins clattering against the metal chute. Music.

Sometimes, one, once six, sometimes two or three fell. She'd scoop them into her palm, using three fingers, getting heart flutters at the music. She had never in her life received something for nothing. She liked it very much.

Recycling the same coins, she amused herself thoroughly all afternoon. Feeling quite elated, she walked through drizzle back to her hotel room. She spread out her pocketful of coins on the bedside table and counted that she had twenty-four twopence pieces over her original pound.

She felt so outlandish that she wondered if she'd need to confess the afternoon's activity to the parish priest at her next confession. It was such fun, it seemed as though it must be a sin.

Shortly Jim returned and they dined out at a Chinese

restaurant; neither enjoyed the food in case a cat or dog had been cooked inside.

During the night she heard the whistle of the Holyhead Mail.

Early the next morning they caught the boat train at Euston, which took them to Holyhead to the boat that took them to Dun Laoghaire, then the train that took them home.

Six weeks later someone named Christie sent her a bank cheque for £2,600. The letter explained that this was the net proceeds from the sale of her collection of letters written by and to Lucia Joyce and three essays, two short, one long and unfinished, written during the past twenty-four years. She showed the cheque to her Jim. With sparkles in his eyes he told her that Miss Joyce had in her own way bequeathed them central heating to keep them cozy in their old age.

Mrs. Leary had no idea who had paid that kind of money for the ramblings of an overmedicated old woman. She had always seen Miss Joyce's special spark and loved her, but she imagined that whoever had paid such a large amount of money for her writings would be terribly disappointed when they read them through. Would they be able to demand the money back? She confessed her anxiety to her priest.

Let the big-headed professors ponder over Miss Joyce's squiggles if they wanted, she thought, eventually giddy at the idea of central heating. Then briefly she regretted that no other of the hundreds of the patients she had cared for over the years had a famous father like James Joyce. Every one of her patients—unless stiff in catatonia—had had the capacity to fill reams and reams of paper with individual ramblings. As she'd always said, appendicitis and cancer are all the same, but no two mentally ill people are alike. That is why she had enjoyed nursing all those years.

With only a few more famous fathers, Jim Leary could have taken a busload of paper to Christie's and she would have died a rich woman. In passing she regretted also that she hadn't done it years before, in time to provide Shee-lagh, her only daughter, with the kind of wedding she'd read about in *You Magazine: Ireland's Review for Woman Today.* Sheelagh was a mother of three of her own. It was too late for a grand wedding.

The euphoria passed and a feeling of emptiness fluttered in her belly; she wouldn't now have dear Lucia Joyce's papers as a special keepsake for her old age. She had imagined reading them and letting the foreign words roll across her tongue in front of the fire on long winter nights as a way of making the time exotically pass. In her life she had only been out of Ireland two times. Lucia had truly lived and carried the cross of worldliness to prove it. It would have been nice, on winter nights, to borrow a whiff of the foreign, whose musty odor wafted up from all of Lucia's jottings, letters, and good manners.

Mr. and Mrs. Leary moved away to Athenry, County Galway, to a small, centrally heated retirement cottage, and until her death from a motoring accident in 1979, she faithfully wrote to Lucia on every second Tuesday and never realized that the erotic love letters that her Jim had written to her had been mixed in with the parcel sold at

Christie's and would probably confuse them for another three hundred years.

A new charge nurse arrived on St. Monica's Ward. The new charge nurse was named Miss Kennedy. She had recently returned home after twenty-five years in America. She was funny and friendly and people said she was quite rich. Lucia liked her. Unfortunately, she had come back sounding like an American in her speech and was very hard to understand. Lucia remembered Americans that had come to call on her father in Paris. She couldn't remember if she had had difficulty understanding their lazy speech as well.

A new popular biography of her father was published, and his collected letters as well, also new critical editions of his work were being prepared for the following year. A copy of the new biography was sent to Lucia. She read in it that James Joyce had been cursed by having an insane daughter. She showed Miss Kennedy the section of the biography about herself. "Do you think it's true?" she asked her.

Miss Kennedy replied, "Surely not. Don't be silly. You know how foreign journalists sensationalize things to get people to buy books."

She read on that the daughter's illness had contributed greatly to Joyce's early demise and to the period of dark despair at the end of his life; that he was responsible for his daughter's illness. The fact that he stopped writing after his last great work was also blamed on his daughter. That their finances had been written about Lucia prayed that her mother would never know.

Then she read that her father had written love letters to a Jewish woman in Zürich that were sold at auction by the woman's sister.

At first she couldn't catch her breath, then she concluded that the book must really be about Father's brother Charles, the one who moved to Massachusetts in America and was a bill sticker. She hadn't known that Uncle Charles had a daughter who had been mentally ill. What a pity. Had she known she would have gladly written to her often and sent cigarettes when she could.

"When my parents come for a visit," she told Miss Kennedy, "don't let them see these scurrilous books."

The writers of yet another scholarly monograph arrived to interview Lucia Joyce. She now called them biografiends, as had her father.

Lucia's health had been declining. She spent many hours of each day in a wheelchair, often asleep, out of doors if the weather was good so that she could listen to the birds sing to her. She seemed to be waiting for someone to arrive, taking special care of her hair each day and donning an old evening gown even in the chill when she had to cover it with the fur jacket and a lap throw.

It was on a beautiful April day that these three scholars came to Barnaderg Bay to interview her for their paper.

The professors gathered around her wheelchair, holding three kinds of tape recorders, and spoke with her in oily tones as though they were coaxing a rather stupid camel through the eye of a needle, offering biscuits first. "Walker's Shortbread Rounds, Miss Joyce? Pure butter. Creamy buttery ummm." They handed her a fistful of biscuits. "Ummm, yummy umm," the coaxing was almost a hum.

Then Miss Joyce started to hum, her voice sweet but erratic. Three hands pounced upon tape recorders, pressing all buttons to "record." One professor named Gogarty held out a Marlboro cigarette.

At this instant she turned coy, tilted her head, batted her eyelashes. *"Pour moi?"* she asked.

All three leaned their faces almost against hers. "Miss Joyce, do you remember anything at all of your father?" one demanded, tape recorder in hand.

"Écoutez!" she ordered.

They dared not breathe.

Her voice dropped into a monotonous tone, quite without affect. "Kale or cabbage? Chop well warm leeks onion tops. UMMMM. Green white summer cream cover soft drain potatoes season. I must."

She spoke more slowly, "Eat leaks milk how. Now. Kale beat pale green fluff. Flame. Deep warm dish. Deep well in center. Pour melted butter. Really I must." She sighed deeply, "Fill up cavity. I must really."

"What papers did your father leave in the rue des Vignes flat when he fled to Switzerland when the Germans came?" one asked her intensely.

She studied the plain biscuit-tin top, *"L'Esclammadore!* Plain gold ring sixpence thimble button bonfire ghosts witches walk abroad. I get the ring."

She thumped one of the men with her forearm. "Are you married?"

He nodded.

"Father opened the big horse's belly. Mother sewed me up inside. I'll be getting married too. Don't rub your mushy fat worm between my thighs again, monsieur. I get the ring."

She spoke no more. She had forgotten him. The cigarette she had been given burned between her lips. Not inhaled. Not exhaled.

The one named Gogarty resisted an urge to squeeze her big old woman's breasts to make her speak again.

She shut her eyes and sweetly whistled a melancholy tune, her whistle intermingling with a mockingbird's trilling sound.

Then she began to snooze.

The three moved off together to the edge of the emerald lawn. Excitement stood out in beads of sweat on all three foreheads. Gogarty rewound his tape, then jammed his long finger against the button. The sound of a mockingbird first, then his voice with the words "Umm, yummy um," and then a mindless hum followed by a second hum. "Strange, I don't think of mockingbirds in Ireland," mused Gogarty.

His associate looked up and removed his eyeglasses.

Not another word was said until the tape had concluded.

"What do you think?" asked the associate, pulling on the end of his nose.

Gogarty made some notes on a small pad and then drew a circle around his notes. "L'Esclammadore! Father's nickname during the early Italian years. The other, colcannon, no doubt. Druidic Sun God feast. Saman, the Lord of Death, that type of thing, bringing together all evil souls who have been condemned for all eternity to inhabit the bodies of wild animals. Also identified as the Irish Saman vigil, Oiche Shamhna. Get it? In my eisegetical view, a tea party. Nausicaa!"

His eyes bulged out of his face.

The other two neither concurred nor disagreed but remained silent.

Gogarty continued, ". . . cabbage and potato dish served up on the last night of October. All Saints' Day, Hallowmass vigil. If you get the sixpence, you'll find wealth, the thimble gets to stay a spinster, the button getter destined to be a bachelor, the ring getter . . . marriage within the year. Could she possibly have any marriage prospects whatsoever?" His tone was mocking.

The third said, "That tune. Hum it again."

The associate tried.

Gogarty spoke, "*Tannhäuser* . . . from Wagner, from the melody sung by Wolfram urging Tannhäuser to return home to Elisabeth, the heartbroken maiden pining for him, the niece of Hermann, Landgrave of Thuringia. You see Joyce hated Wagner but his wife liked Wagner."

Gogarty went on, "An orgy figures prominently in this act of the opera. Sexual fantasy about the father . . . that would concur with my interpretation of the missing letters from 1922, the other notebooks, my theory will be proved when the two wagonloads of papers and books are unsealed in 1991 . . ." He licked his lips. "I'm sure it'll match up exactly to my incestuous interpretations of the

Scribbledehobble notebook I outlined in my paper at Milan, 1969.''

He turned on the tape recorder and listened to the humming duet again.

If he hadn't known better he would have sworn that the bird and Lucia were conducting a duet.

He held degrees from three universities. He knew better.

A confetti of swallows swept willy-nilly across the rolling lawn. Their closeness to the ground usually predicted rain. Gogarty noticed that a small man had begun the long walk up the gravel drive from the iron gate. At a distance he looked like someone who had been to the opera. Gogarty couldn't resist laughing.

He saw that Miss Joyce had risen up from her chair at the sight of him; her fur and lap robe had fallen to the ground, and she stood in a lovely, iridescent silver-and-green evening gown. She seemed to be either laughing or whistling at the sight of him too.

Author's Afterword

THE AUTHOR acknowledges that apart from biographical facts, Lucia Joyce is a product of the imagination, with an imagined inner life. In creating her the author has drawn upon the many well-known details from the lives of the Joyce family, their contemporaries, and the times in which they lived.

The author has tossed a salad using the scholarship of others and acknowledges D. Bair, S. Beach, B. B. Delimata, R. Ellmann, L. Gillet, D. Hayman, A. Hoffmeister, J. Lidderdale, B. Maddox, J. Mercanton, I. Nadel, M. Nicholson, among many.

Great care has been taken to respect the private and personal lives of the subjects. No use has been made of medical records or of intimate letters that invade family privacy. The course of Miss Joyce's illness after 1935 has been largely imagined.

Although she was diagnosed as schizophrenic, James Joyce, unlike his wife, for many years refused to accept the fact that his daughter was sick. Instead he believed that she was clairvoyant and a genius like himself. James and Nora Joyce protected her as long as they could, until the gathering cataclysm of World War II swept across their fates and they could protect her no longer.

James Joyce died suddenly in Zürich in 1941. Nora Joyce also died in Zürich, in 1951. She never saw her daughter after the war. Giorgio Joyce died in Konstanz, Germany, in 1976. He visited Lucia once, in 1967. The three share a grave at Fluntern Cemetery in Zürich.

After forty-seven years in asylums in France, Switzerland, and England, Lucia Joyce died in the geriatric ward of St. Andrew's Hospital in Northampton, England, on December 12, 1982.

Despite an empty grave in Zürich beside her parents and brother, Lucia lies buried at Kingsthorpe Cemetery, her grave shaded by a chestnut tree as was her wish.

This book salutes her ability to survive in the grip of a most mysterious and terrible illness and is dedicated to the sad, thwarted fate of so many who are struck down by mental illness, as well as to all kind, caring nurses around the world especially Nurse A. G. Kennedy of Dublin and New York, whose loving care altered this author's life.

Barnaderg Bay Hospital is wholly imaginary and bears no resemblance to any institution in Ireland or anywhere else. Mrs. Leary, Edgar Anthagros, among others, are residents of the author's imagination and bear no resemblance to persons living or dead.

Lucia Joyce did not have red hair.

Notes

1. "Thanks be to God for this miracle. After twenty years I see the light once more."
2. "Socrates and His Disciples Mocked by the Courtesans."
3. "There was a little girl who laughed during the day and did not sleep at night."
4. The green fairy.
5. The White Tower.
6. Intensely observant gaze.
7. "The sea-cat and death-strangling."
8. "Praying! Withering!"
9. Imbecile.